DESIRE FOR
Love

MASSIMO PARLERMO

PAGE PUBLISHING, INC.
Conneaut Lake, PA

First originally published by Page Publishing 2021

ISBN 978-1-6624-3305-4 (pbk)
ISBN 978-1-6624-3306-1 (digital)

Printed in the United States of America

INTRODUCTION

This is a story about a man trying to find a woman to settle down with and start a family, and although this seemingly is a simple idea, it is much harder for some people to find the one for them than it is for others. This can be attributed to many different factors, to a person finding what he or she is looking for, or sometimes it may be something that the individual has no control of. This story follows a man named Gianni Martino and takes place over four decades of his life, and this story digs into his life and experiences and his struggles. The story starts when he is in grammar school when he was trying to break out of his painfully shy personality and then takes you to a more recent period into his middle ages and trying to take everything that he learned through his life to try to apply it to today's life and society as we know it. The story takes you through the many stages of Gianni growing up from a young, shy boy to a mature man and the many incredible tales that he went through and experienced. For most people, any one of the stories he experienced would be a once-in-a-lifetime event for them, but for Gianni these stories happened time after time, and he never had to lift a finger or be the initiator to make such things happen to him.

Throughout his life, he kept trying to understand or figure out what it was that caused these events to occur to him, but that was a great mystery never meant to be solved. A little background about Gianni Martino: he was a man who grew up in Chicago, and as he was growing up through the years, he was always complimented as a cute boy by girls his own age as well as older ladies, who would also compliment him as a handsome man. He grew up with a complex about his looks, and as a matter of fact he was very modest about his good looks, and his quiet demeanor certainly did not help his cause to break out of his shell until he was older. Maybe his quiet and shy personality is what drew the girls to him because they liked the idea of a shy guy, and perhaps that made them feel comfortable around him. Gianni did change his attitude over the years from the heartaches he would endure, and it would be difficult for him to maintain that positive attitude that he would find that one woman for him. But that goal seemed to be out of reach for him especially when he got older and his hopes of finding that special woman in his life seemed to fade away, and he would have to simply accept how things turned out for him. His destiny was already set; he just needed to stop trying to understand or figure out what exactly this destiny was for him.

For one reason or another, Gianni had this effect on people looking after him. Not just his family, his friends also seemed to want to protect him in some way, shape, or form. Seems that someone always had Gianni under their thumb and protecting him, and so that was a big reason he was so shy. Another big reason was, growing up in school he noticed that he was one of the two shorter boys in the class. I am sure you can picture your class school picture where the shortest kids would be sitting toward the front of the stage sitting and holding the plaque to indicate what the year and class was in the photo. Combined with those two reasons of why Gianni was on the shy side, it is not surprising why it would take as long for him to break out of his shell. It was a slow process for him to break out of his shell even as he grew older. When he got older and was able to break out of his shyness, Gianni was able to get dates with women and many of which did not go beyond a first date because Gianni did not want to waste time with a woman he was not going to build a relationship with or felt she was someone that he was interested in building a relationship with. No matter how many dates he had, he always felt lonely, which is exactly how he would feel if he was having sex with a different woman every night. Oh sure, he would get his physical needs taken care of, but at the end of the day he knew he would feel awful lonely with all those different women, so he chose not to live that lifestyle that his friends said they would lead if they looked like him. For Gianni it did not matter what his age was:

whether he was a teenager, a man in his twenties, or a man in his thirties or his forties, the women seemed to always be comfortable around him and be aggressive toward him.

Gianni did not seek attention, but over the years he seemed to always attract attention from friends or family regardless of what he did. He was a shy boy, especially around girls in grade school and high school and early on in college. Although he was shy and quiet, for the most part Gianni made friends easily, and most people liked him because he was a nice guy and he had a great sense of humor and was trustworthy and honest. Most people were impressed by him immediately, and he was the guy that when he met his friend's parents, they would immediately like him and knew he was a good person, and their kids would not get into trouble because of Gianni. He was well-liked by his friends, he was well-liked by his friends' families, and of course he was very well-liked by women. The women who would be aggressive toward him were not ordinary-looking women but very attractive women. Perhaps he had the right look that just seemed to draw women or a combination of good looks and his quiet demeanor that made women comfortable enough to want to approach him, or maybe it was his warm, friendly smile. In any case he would get attention, and the people around him noticed because they never got that same attention that he would. He found a lot of solace from music. Throughout his life, he would remember or associate songs with his past or the recent situations that occurred. Or if at the very moment things were happening to him, he would try to think of the best song he knew that best fit the situation. Many times, when he was driving in his car alone, he would blast his music to get over recent pain or try to recall happier times. And as he grew older, a lot of the songs that would make him feel better about those bad situations were now in fact bringing tears to his eyes. Another common theme for Gianni was not only were women aggressive toward him, but also that they would do it in front of him and his friends or people he worked with. Gianni would be minding his own business at a McDonald's or at a party or in a parking lot or at a health club or on a train—these were just some of the places that he would draw attention.

When his friends would see that women get aggressive with him, they would always react the same way—it seemed that they would either be in disbelief, or one of them would say, "Why doesn't something like that ever happen to me?" He was not the captain of the football team, he was not a celebrity or famous, and he was not a person in power. But that did not matter for Gianni at any stage in his life. And those things did not matter to a woman being aggressive toward him. And it did not matter what the age of the woman was, or if she was older than him, or if she was ten years or twenty years younger than him for that matter. He would still garner this attention and aggressiveness from women. It did not matter where he should happen to be or who was with him. If he was standing in an elevator or was sitting in a restaurant with his friends or at a grocery store parking lot, it was the same. In some ways Gianni caused problems for others, even though he did not initiate the trouble. He was not a confrontational person, but somehow conflict would follow him wherever he went. Just because he was out on a date with a woman did not mean that it would stop a waitress or a female patron to flirt with him, which in turn would upset the woman he was with on the date.

Another common theme, it seemed, was that his friends or coworkers would see these things happen in front of their very own eyes, and in many ways these things that happened to him became legendary among his friends and family. And in many ways he became a legend, and Giannis's friends saw him in action or would witness the events that made him a legend. They would always seem to ask him the same question or make the same comments, like "How come that never happens to me" or "How do you do that?" Gianni never had a really good answer to those questions because even he was surprised by what continuously occurred to him over the years. For Gianni, women seem to swarm toward him, and the guys would either envy him or be outright jealous because their woman was checking him out or talking about him. When the guys were envious of him sometimes, they would tell him directly to his face or indirectly. Indirectly one of them would say, for example, "Oh a guy that looks like Gianni probably sleeps with a new girl every day," and of course directly one of them would say something to the effect of "Gianni, if I had your looks and your body, I would be sleeping with a different girl every day!" Well, if Gianni wanted, maybe he could have had a different girl daily or frequently as his friends suggested, but he was not looking for that kind of lifestyle and that just was not who he was. He wanted to lead a very simple lifestyle; he wanted something very similar with what he grew up with. He wanted to be a husband and a father and have a wife and kids. For him that would have made him happy, and that is what he wanted out of life. He did not seek or want the other lifestyles his friends said they would have led if they were him.

CHAPTER 1

Gianni attended Jacques Grammar School, and for the most part most of his friends were the kids he went to school with and grew up with. Gianni became friends with a new girl named Renee. It turned out that by the time they graduated Jacques Grammar School, she became the most popular girl in the class: class president, prettiest girl in school, the absolute dream girl, a parent's dream of a smart and popular student, a schoolboy's first crush, and so forth. Gianni was shy because he was the youngest of three brothers, and so he had the pressure of being the youngest and knowing the least or had the least amount of experience, so he had his older brothers always looking out after him even when Mom and Dad were not looking after him. The attention he began to receive started for him during his eighth-grade school year at Jacques School.

This was the year that he noticed some changes in himself and the way people acted around him. He noticed his physical changes that developed. As he was growing up, he was one of the shorter kids in the class, year after year, that was until he sprung up and grew in height and was no longer one of the shorter kids in class! He was not the tallest, but he was no longer the shortest and was incredibly happy for sure. One of the first things he did was he asked Renee if she would do him a favor and line up with him back to back to confirm his newfound height! She asked him why he asked her to line up with him, and he told her that since the third grade she was always taller than him and wanted to confirm that he was now taller than her and must have gotten that growth spurt over the summer. And now that he confirmed he was taller than Renee, he began to start feeling confident about himself! Not only was Gianni cute, but now he was also tall! Gianni was getting tall and confident, and lo and behold he got the best news he could get for his last year in grammar school before he would be starting high school—he would get to sit behind Renee during class, his new neighbor in class. He was practically gloating from happiness because the other boys in class, well, let's just say what he got was the most coveted seat.

As Gianni was beginning to mature, his friends must have started to notice or feel he was a competition for Renee, which was kind of ironic since none of the boys were making their moves on her!

For the most part, Gianni kept to himself. He would have conversations and talk with everyone in school, and although quiet he would call people out if their bullshit was just too much. And although he was a quiet individual, he would not back down. In one such instance, one day a group of the guys from class were having lunch and talking. One of the guys, Ronnie, was going on and talking very boastfully that he had gone out on dates with lots of girls already, and he could have any choice of girls he wanted at Jacques School because he was the best-looking guy in the eighth grade.

Some of the guys were getting a little annoyed by his talking, including Gianni. Gianni said, "Ronnie, you need to get off your high horse, dude!"

Ronnie said, "Oh yeah? Who is better looking than me? What, you think you are better looking than me?"

So of course, some of the other guys were egging Ronnie on, and Gianni was taken aback by Ronnie's challenge, since it came out of left field because Gianni was not even suggesting or bragging that he was the better-looking guy in class. And he certainly was not expecting this talk to come from his friends. Then all of a sudden, some of the other guys began to suggest confirming who is the better looking of the two by simply asking the hottest girl in class, Renee!

Oh boy, that was not what Gianni wanted to hear. All of a sudden they were having this discussion, but the last thing he wanted to hear was that Renee would say anything less of him, whether it was his looks or him in general. After all, they had been friends since the third grade. She was one of his Gianni's oldest friends in school, and this would be so very embarrassing to him. But it would also be devasting to him if he were to hear her say anything bad about him from her.

The guys wanted to get the answer once and for all, and so they dared Ronnie and the rest of the group to go ask Renee. And they all finally walked over to Renee, although Gianni wasn't exactly thrilled about the idea of going up to her and putting her on the spot by asking for her opinion. But at this point, they were going to ask her whether he wanted them to ask her or not.

And sure enough, Ronnie the big mouth began to speak, and not surprisingly Renee wasn't expecting all of the guys to come over and ask her the burning question, "Renee, who is better looking, Ronnie or Gianni?"

Renee was shocked by the question and almost fell out of her chair, but she answered quickly and said that Gianni was cuter! Ronny turned and then responded with "Oh she only said Gianni because they sit so close to each other." And everyone dispersed and walked back to their desk. Of course, Gianni was so delighted with her answer but had to control his emotions since he sat so close to her, and he did not care why she said it, and he also looked at it as two positives. First this would shut up Ronnie the big mouth, and second also knowing that Renee thinks that Gianni is cute was just the icing on the cake for him!

After school was over and everyone was heading out to their lockers, Renee got up from her desk and turned to Gianni and asked, "Why were you guys asking me who was better looking?"

Gianni told her he had no idea how the topic even came up but that Ronnie was talking a lot of trash about how he was the best-looking guy in class. "And so I called him out on that told him he needed to get off his ego trip, and then he responded by saying, "Oh, who is better looking than me, you think you are?' And all of a sudden, before I knew it, Ronnie and the rest of those other guys felt they needed to confirm who was the best-looking guy in class, and apparently it was either Ronnie or yours truly. And there was only one person in class who could be the final decision, and that person was you, Renee."

He could always associate the song "Cool It Now" by New Edition with Renee. His class was having a class pizza party, and that song was playing in the background. She walked over to Gianni when this song was playing, and they were speaking to each other, and he would always think about Renee whenever he heard that song playing. She would be attending a Catholic high school in the burbs as Gianni would be attending a public school in Chicago, Belmont High School. And so he didn't know when he would ever see Renee or many other of his friends, since a few of them would be moving to the suburbs during the summer to avoid going to Belmont High.

The school he would be attending had a reputation about being rough and tough, and a lot of his closest friends had a fear of going there, but there would be a friend or two of his that would be going to school with him. Although it was a large school, he probably would not see them much, so another adjustment was coming for Gianni. Gianni never asked Renee out for several reasons, but the main reason was that he was very shy at that point in his life, and asking a girl out was not an easy thing to do. And also, there was the fact that he had not entered into the dating scene—that was another reason.

Another reason was that, although he knew Renee thought he was cute, he was not confident she liked him to go out on a date. Graduation came, and everybody wished each other well and said goodbye to one another. Gianni knew there would be at least two of his classmates he would see in the fall when high school started, but he began to get sad for he thought this would be the last time he would ever see Renee.

During the summer break between graduating Jacques School and starting his high school freshman year, he was enjoying his freedom from not having homework, watching baseball, playing sports himself, and just trying to adjust to his maturity and mentally preparing for what would be a tough transition to high school. His mother and his sisters insisted that he go with them to the mall to do some shopping for his school clothes, and he was none too pleased with this idea. But he knew he really didn't have a choice but to go. There he was out at the mall with his mother and two sisters, and he really had no interest in hanging out with them. He would rather be home watching a Cubs game rather than be there in public with them, but he was promised that they were going to do some shopping for clothes for the fall semester, and it would be a very quick trip to the mall. So he begrudgingly agreed to tag along.

This might have taught him a big lesson that there is no such thing as a quick trip to the mall! It turned out to be a disaster for him. First of all, the focus was squarely on Mom and his sisters, so he was getting agitated that he was even there with them. And as the girls continued to try out all kinds of outfits going in and out of store after store, it seemed this trip to the mall was never going to end. And then they decided to check out one last store, and so he decided not to enter with them and told them he would wait for them in the mall by the middle where there was seating available to sit.

Sitting there, he began to scan the mall to check out who was there, if there were any of his friends at the same time as he was. He didn't see any, so he was escaping the embarrassment of being with his sisters and mother at the mall. Suddenly, he noticed a couple girls in his age group walking toward his direction, and he began to get this gut feeling that something was about to happen.

As he was sitting there, he was checking out his wristwatch, which was digital. The options he had were the twenty-four-hour military-style time or the regular twelve-hour time because he was getting nervous about the two girls he saw walking. As he started to look up, waiting on his family to come out of the store, he noticed the two girls walking toward where he was sitting. He suddenly began to realize that his disaster of a day was about to reach another level when he started thinking, *Oh my god, these girls are going to stop and sit right by the empty spaces next to me.*

He began to get even more nervous and scared and started staring down at his watch, changing it back and forth between the twenty-four hours to twelve hours and so forth. Sure enough, the girls did sit down next to him, and now he really didn't know what to do. His sisters and mother were just a few feet away, and he felt like if he made a move they would walk up to him right as he was in the middle of his move and embarrass the hell out of him. As he sat and stared down at his watch and thought about what his next move would be, the girl sitting closest to him started up a conversation with Gianni and said to him, "Do you have the time?"

Wow, Gianni was in shock that the girl made the first move. He then proceeded to tell her the time and got up and left and walked over to the store and began to tell his mom and sisters that they needed to go home now! He felt he missed out an opportunity, and yes, he sure did. He probably could have simply said to her after giving the time, "I need to go, but can I have your phone number?" But he was too scared and shy to ask for it. When he got home, he began to analyze the situation and thought back and then thought to himself, *She asked me if I have the time. My goodness, this girl was practically throwing herself at me. No doubt I would have gotten my first-ever phone number from a girl.*

Gianni associated this encounter with the song "I Ran (So Far Away)" by A Flock of Seagulls. He definitely ran away from the girls that had just sat down to speak with him and struck up a conversation.

CHAPTER 2

His freshman year at Belmont High turned out to be a quiet time with the girls in his life. He was just getting his feet wet and adapting to high school in general. It was definitely a big change from Jacques School. Many of the friends he made at Jacques School would not be attending the same high school as Gianni, because most of his friends decided to move or go to private schools, and the few classmates from Jacques School that he was friends with that attended Belmont High were not in any of his classes or lunch or study breaks. Two of his classmates from Jacques, Glen and Rick, tried to continue on with their friendship by meeting every morning at Glen's house and then walking to Belmont High. But since they had to go their own separate ways with different classes in their schedule, they only saw each other at the very beginning of the day, and as time went on through the semester, they got distant from each other.

And so now Gianni found himself a little bit separated from Jacques School and had to make new friends. And yes, he managed to make some new friends. He found it odd that none of his classmates from Jacques were in his classes or that he never ran into them in the halls, but Belmont High was a very large school—four floors of classrooms, and there was a large student body attending. Although he made an attempt to keep the friendships going, at Jacques it just never materialized. A couple guys he befriended were Perry and Tim. They were in the same physical education class and a couple other classes together, and they began hanging out during their study breaks and lunch breaks and then after school.

The guys began to bond by playing basketball or football after school, and they all were also focused on which girl they should pursue. They also were working on expanding their three-person friend group to a larger group overall. There were all kinds of characters that managed to latch on to the original three guys, and all had something to add to the mix. The overall theme was that all the guys were not friends for a long time, and they were all getting to learn about one another. It was interesting to see those that claimed they had experience with girls. Gianni was not too sure what to really believe, but he would just listen to what they were saying and see if he could learn something.

All he knew was that he has had some interesting things happen to him since the eighth grade, but he still had not stepped up to the plate to ask a girl out. And he was not only trying to get the nerve to finally ask a girl out, but he was also adjusting to a new school, new friends, and essentially a new life from what he had been used to. As was tradition with Gianni, he sat back and observed and tried to make the best of the situation. He felt that thinking positive would be a good way to emit good energy and thus get good results.

As they headed into the summer break after their freshman year at Belmont High, Perry mentioned to Gianni that he had a date with a girl but that she also had a friend who wanted a date also. Perry recommended to her his good friend Gianni, and he was responsible for Giannis's first blind date. And boy, did it turn out to be a doozy of a date, not just for Gianni but also for the both of them. Gianni accepted the offer to go out on this blind date, figuring that this might be a good way to at least get a little experience under his belt. He could now say he had been out on a date, and he would have his new good friend, Perry, by his side just so that would eliminate all the pressure that goes with being out on first date.

It was a simple date. They all hung out at the local ice-cream shop and sat and talked and then did some walking around as well. Gianni wasn't very happy with his date. He didn't find her attractive, and she was much taller than Gianni, so it made for an uncomfortable evening for Gianni. Plus, she was annoying, constantly complaining throughout the night, and even complained she didn't want an ice-cream cone because it would be a subconscious notion of her licking a man's penis. Gianni could not believe that someone could continue to not just whine and complain all night, but also manage to get more annoying while she was doing it. Gianni looked at Perry to indicate that he was about to blow his top! Gianni could not wait for this evening to end, and he could hear in his head the song "Ride Like the Wind" by Christopher Cross.

He so badly wanted to get out of this evening, and this song was saying to him to ride like the wind. Gianni felt how appropriate this song was so he could take his mind off the evening, even for just a few moments. The evening came to an end, and Gianni headed home. He did not seek a hug or kiss, or even a handshake for that matter.

The next day, Perry gave him a call, and Gianni told him to never ask him for a favor like that again. Perry swore that he didn't know the girl and had no idea what she looked like. That he had never met her and had no idea what her personality was like. And if he had known, he wouldn't have put him and himself through that because he too wasn't exactly having fun thanks to Miss Sunshine!

Gianni told Perry that he did not blame him, but he should be a little more careful the next time a girlfriend or date asks for him to get a friend for her friend. Perry was very sorry for the disastrous evening and that if it made him feel any better, he probably would not see his date again either. It was his first date for Perry with the girl he was out with, and he told Gianni that she told him she would only go out on a date with him if he got one of his friends to tag along for her friend. Gianni felt bad that it was also a bad night for Perry and told him maybe next time that they were out on dates it would be a more pleasant evening.

During his sophomore year at Belmont High, Gianni was comfortable and adjusted to high school, so he was much more comfortable with his settings, with his friends, and with his surroundings— the life of high school as he just learned about in his freshman year. Once the fall semester started, he noticed a girl from freshmen class, and she certainly drew his attention. He got very much interested in this freshman girl from study hall break. There she was with her long blond hair, bright blue eyes, and a nice shape that seemed to combine perfect to Gianni. Day after day he would notice and see her sitting with her friend at another table, and his friends Perry and

Tim noticed that Gianni always seemed to be distracted while they were speaking to him. Like he was staring or looking and checking someone out at another table. They finally figured out who had caught his interest.

Perry and Tim began to tease Gianni, telling him things like "Hey, you like that girl. Why don't you go over to her and say something?" to this girl that he had taken an interest in. Then of course they were not going to let this go until he made his move on the girl, and they kept ragging on him and daring him to go or calling him a pussy unless he walked over to her and make his move.

Finally, after a few days and after enough teasing and building up enough nerve, Gianni told Perry and Tim that he was going to do it, and they continued to tease him, and one of them said to him, "Yeah right, sure you will."

Gianni then said, "Oh yeah? Watch this." And he got up and walked over toward her table as each step he took he could hear in his head the song "Fresh" by Kool & the Gang. Or was that his heartbeat pounding very loudly? Because he could not hear anything in the outside world, only in his mind and heart, as his friends looked on excitedly to see him finally walk over to her and see how things would turn out for him. Finally he reached her table and began to introduces himself to the mystery girl he'd seen daily.

He did it. He said hello and introduced himself to her. And although she told Gianni that her name was Katrina, she seemed hesitant to tell him her name and did not seem to want to talk with him nor look at him as she spoke. She looked at her friend as if to say, "Oh my god, I hope he leaves soon" as Gianni was speaking to her.

He tried to ask her questions to get her engaged in the conversation as he continued to try and find out about her as much as he could, like what grade school she graduated from, whereabouts in the city did she live, little things to have a conversation. She was very reluctant to share much information to him, and her answers were short and sweet. She seemed to be telling her friend as she was answering his questions. He did not want to believe she did not like him and thought her responses were due the fact that maybe she was shy or scared, or that she was a freshman, and so forth. The bell rang and study hall was over, and he said goodbye to Katrina and headed back to his friends. They asked him how it went, and he told them he would give them the details during lunch and that he had to get to his next class. The guys were still happy that Gianni walked over to talk to her no matter the results!

Lunchtime arrived, and he gave the details to his buddies, and they were impressed. One of them told him, "She told you her name, and she didn't tell you to get lost or drop dead? You are in good shape. You broke the ice!"

Gianni told the guys that he had been thinking about it since study hall was over, and he did not think it went well. He felt that he was getting the cold shoulder from her. She did not seem very happy he was there, like he was interrupting her conversation with her friend.

Then Perry and Tim said, "Hey, girls always play hard to get. You know that, right?"

And Gianni said, "Play hard to get?"

"Oh, sure girls like guys to win them over. You know, they like to look like they are not interested but want you to continue to win her over."

Then one of them continued and said, "Look, we were watching you when you walked over to her. Dude, we were like a fly on the wall. She likes you, man, no doubt."

He walked over to her again the next day and again got some more of the same reluctant attitude, and the conversation was just as bad as the day before. The bell rang again, and he headed back toward his friends. One of them said, "Good job, Gianni, you are wearing her down now."

He said, "Wearing her down? I don't want to wear someone down. I think I am going to try a different approach next, but I'll have to explain what I mean later. Got to get to class."

Lunch arrived again, and Gianni said, "Look, you guys said I need to win her over. And I don't think me talking to her is doing much. I found out where her locker is."

And one of them said, "So what if you know where her locker is?"

Gianni then said, "I will write her some poems and letters and try to sweep her off her feet that way!"

"Oh look at good ole Romeo here," one of the boys said to him, and Gianni laughed and said, "Well, I am Italian," and they all laughed.

In the meanwhile, Perry and Tim were scheming on playing a little joke on Gianni. They felt that writing her poems would fail miserably. They were correct. She was not receptive to the messages. One time, Gianni waited around the corner from the locker after he left her a message. He saw that she read it, and he then saw her crumple up the note and toss it in the nearby garbage. Ouch, that hurt him and made him sad. He finally concluded that he must not have been the type of guy she liked, although he had no clue as to what that type it was that she liked.

Gianni told the guys that he was done pursuing Katrina and should focus on a girl that liked him or would at least talk to him! And Perry and Tim and the rest of the guys completely agreed with him, and then Perry said, "Oh by the way, I got this last period from a friend of a friend of a friend who told me to give this to you the next time I saw you," and so he handed him an envelope.

This was that little prank Perry and Tim were working on to play on Gianni. Gianni was puzzled by getting a note and then began reading the note. He could smell the scent of perfume from the note and noticed a girl's handwriting on the note. He began to read it, and it was a love note stating how she was crazy in love with him and that she was too shy to say anything to him. But he has not even noticed her yet, and it was signed his secret admirer with a lipstick impression of a kiss at the end. Gianni started pushing Perry for more information on this note, and said to Perry, "Okay who wrote this?"

Gianni was not buying it for one moment, and Perry was like "Dude, I swear I don't know who wrote it" and then laughed and said that he didn't wear that kind of perfume!

"Come on, give it up, Perry. You know who wrote this. A friend of a friend of a friend? Are you kidding me? I don't buy it for one minute. I think you know exactly who wrote this, and you are fucking with me!"

Perry said, "I don't know who wrote it, I swear. Maybe it's one of your sister's friends. You see how they act around you, they get all giddy."

"Oh really?" Gianni said. "Well, if it was one of my sister's friends, why didn't *my sister give me the note*? Remember the note said I had not even noticed her. Well, it's not like I have ignored my sister's friends. So they are eliminated from being the secret admirer."

Perry and Tim were surprised that Gianni was not buying that the note was legitimate. One of them then said, "Why don't you believe us that you have a secret admirer and it's legitimate?"

Gianni said, "If you guys wanted me to buy this bullshit, the least you could have done was slip the note in my locker. Then maybe I might have given it a second thought. But the timing of the note, the fact that you happened to have a note right after I tell you I was done with Katrina. And if it was legitimate that the girl who wrote the note would had given it to you, Perry, and then you could had said this girl gave it to me."

Perry responded with "What, come on, that note was written by a girl. Look at the letter."

And Gianni said, "Yeah, sure, it was written by a girl. You probably asked one of the Verdi twin sisters to write this letter but not to tell you which girl actually wrote the letter. That way you can have deniability to say you don't know who wrote the letter!"

Tim said, "*Holy shit*, how did you do that? How did you figure this it out so quick?"

Gianni said, "You guys are messing with the wrong guy. I smell bullshit a mile away. I smelled it before I even read the note."

Tim laughed and said, "That was the perfume you smelled," and they all laughed.

Perry then said, "No, but seriously, how did you figure it out so quick?"

Gianni told them that, although they'd only known each other a little over a year, he already knew their style, and this was a prank that would be right up their alley!

After the disappointing pursuance of his blond dream and the failed joke of a secret admirer in the first semester, Gianni then started paying more attention to a classmate from his history class. Her name was Natalie, and she was the opposite of Katrina. She was a brunette with dark eyes and actually spoke to Gianni and gave him the time of the day. She was friendly with him, she sat in the seat in front of him, and in many ways her personality was a lot like Renee from Jacques School. Every day he seemed to get to like her more and more. What a wasted first couple months pursuing Katrina, when all along here was Natalie. She was in his class, and she was in his afternoon study hall period, and they would wave hello when they saw each other in study hall.

She waved hello to him in the halls when they walked past each other, and he started feeling a friendship developing, but to his disappointment he found out she had a boyfriend. She mentioned it during a conversation in class to him, and Gianni thought he should not try to put the moves on her. He began telling Perry and Tim about Natalie and told them how hot she was. The next time he'd see her at study hall, he would point her out to them.

Perry and Tim began to ask. "Well, what are you waiting for? Why don't you ask her out?"

Gianni said, "Don't you guys pay attention to details? She has a boyfriend, so she is off limits!"

They began to start giving him a difficult time, and the teasing began as was tradition with these guys. They said he was just making excuses to not ask her out because he was chicken shit! Or maybe because he fell flat on his face with Katrina. Or she was not hot at all, or this girl was totally made up!

One day during study hall, Natalie walked by the table where Gianni and Perry and Tim were sitting, and they said hello to each other. Then she continued to walk over to her table, where her friends were sitting. Perry and Tim asked Gianni who that was, and he said, "Who was that? Well, that is Natalie."

They both responded, "That is the Natalie you've been telling us about?"

Gianni said, "Yeah, why?"

Tim and Perry both said, "Dude. She is hot!"

Gianni laughed and said, "Yeah, I know. I told you that already. What do you think, I would say she was hot when she was not?"

Perry responded with "Yeah, but dude she's *hot*. And she said hello to you. And she is real!"

Gianni told the guys, "Yeah of course she said hello to me. I told you I'd been talking with her. What do you think, I made up the fact that I was talking with a hot girl?"

The guys seemed shocked that Natalie was giving Gianni the time of day. And of course, Perry just could not let Gianni enjoy the moment for awfully long, and he would have to somehow embarrass Gianni at some point. That some point came along a couple days later when Gianni, Perry, and Tim were all sitting in their afternoon study hall near the telephone, when lo and behold who comes walking over to use the phone—none other than Natalie. As usual, she smiled and waved to Gianni, and then he returned to his conversation with the guys. But little did he know what Perry had in store for him.

Perry decided to try and be funny and mess with Gianni a tad. As soon as Natalie hung up the phone, Perry yelled out to her, "Excuse me! Could you please come over here? I have a question for you."

And she walked over to their table to see what he wanted to ask her. Gianni was surprised, and he had no idea that Perry was even going to say anything to her. And then he proceeded to ask Natalie, "Is Gianni your boyfriend?"

Tim began laughing. Giannis's mouth nearly dropped to the floor; he was so embarrassed.

Natalie responded to Perry and said, "No, he is not."

Perry turned to Gianni and said, "You liar. She is not your girlfriend!"

Perry and Tim began laughing. While Gianni was trying to utter the words "I never said that," Natalie realized what Perry was up to and then quickly followed up by saying that, well, if she did not already have a boyfriend, she would definitely be Gianni's girlfriend and then walked back to her friends! Tim and Perry's jaws just dropped, and Gianni blushed and turned about three dark shades of red. But he could not stop smiling because of the smackdown Natalie just gave Perry. And then he thought back to Renee, and when Ronnie put her on the spot to ask her who she thought was cuter! Gianni then told Perry, "That will teach you to try to prank me again!" Gianni began to gloat and starting feeling a little special and started thinking about the song "You Made Me Believe in Magic" by the Bay City Rollers, a little flashback to when he was a kid in the 1970s. When the bell rang, Gianni walked over to Natalie to apologize for what Perry did and promised he wasn't telling the guys that she was his girlfriend. Natalie said it was all right, and she saw through what Perry was doing. But she meant what she said that if she wasn't involved, she would be interested in him!

Gianni could not believe his ears. She was not just saying it to shut Perry up and thought Natalie was not only a good friend but also very sweet and nice. He wished she didn't have a boyfriend already because it would be very torturous for Gianni the rest of the semester, knowing that she would want him as a boyfriend. A couple weeks after the study hall incident with Perry, Gianni was in history class, and Natalie was returning from an absence of school from the day before. She turned to Gianni and asked if she had missed anything and if she could copy his notes. He responded that yeah he had notes, but he wasn't sure if they were legible. So she took a look at them and said he was right, she couldn't read his notes.

Another classmate sitting next to Gianni said he had notes, and they were very legible, and she could copy his notes if she wanted. She got up and began to copy down the notes, and as she was writing down the notes, she then all of a sudden decided to use Gianni's thigh as a chair for herself! Gianni nearly had a heart attack. First this girl he was very much attracted to was now making physical contact with him, and secondly Gianni could have had a very embarrassing moment, since he happened to be wearing sweatpants. If he wasn't careful, everyone would notice that he was very excited or turned on to have Natalie sitting on his lap. He luckily managed to keep his excitement to a minimum and didn't have this potentially embarrassing moment!

Gianni was so delighted that she made some physical contact with him that he just could not wait until study hall to share this news with Perry and Tim! Gianni shared the news with the guys, and they could not believe it. One of them said, "Like, dude, how did you manage to get that hot girl to sit on your leg?"

Gianni was like "Dude, I did not do anything. She saw my leg there and decided to use it as a chair! Can I help it? She felt comfortable with me that she could use my leg in that manner? Hey, do you guys think this was a sign or hint to me?"

One of them said, "You said she has a boyfriend, right?"

Gianni said yes, "But just maybe she's done with that guy, and it's my time, Maybe all she needed was me to ask her out, and she would dump his ass!"

Tim was like "Dude, do not get ahead of yourself from someone using your leg as a chair. Haha!"

Gianni could not help but wonder what was going on and began to think about the song "Head Games" from Foreigner. He did not know if she was messing with his head or if it was truly an innocent event. Or was it maybe a subtle hint again by her? After all, she said it not once but twice. If she did not have a boyfriend, she would be interested in Gianni. He did not know what to do. He asked Tim and Perry what they would do. Gianni thought he should wait until it was closer to the end of the semester to ask Natalie out because if she said no, then he would have the summer to recover from the rejection!

Gianni did not make a move with Natalie and never asked her out, probably because he felt she did have a boyfriend and would have to say no for that reason alone. The thing about Natalie was that she came across as genuine and did not seem like someone would make up the fact that she had a boyfriend, plus he felt she was too attractive not to have a boyfriend.

Gianni began working a part-time job during his sophomore year at a pizzeria not too far from Belmont High School and was able to get the job after he met the manager of pizzeria. He was asked if he wanted to work a few hours a week, mainly on the weekends, and they could definitely use some help for the weekends. He took the job, and it was a very close-knit type of atmosphere. Most of the people that worked there were either related to the owner or a friend of the manager, and so it was almost like a second family for Gianni, especially since most of the employees were Italian to start with.

Although the job he held was taking orders for customers and there were several other guys close in proximity to his age, some were either seniors or just entering college age. And when they figured out that Gianni wasn't very experienced with girls, well, they felt it was their duty to get Gianni "laid." They tried to send him girls in the restaurant to see if any of them would catch his eye, but the thing was, Gianni just really wasn't ready to just go all in with any girl just to say he was no longer a virgin. And so he told the guys at the pizzeria to not worry about him and that when the time was right for him it, would just happen. They were also very protective of Gianni, like he was their little brother, and one such example was that Tim had just joined the wrestling team. Gianni told him that since Tim lived so close to the pizzeria, he and some of the guys from the team should stop by after wrestling practice, and he would buy them pizza.

Gianni was also a very generous person. This was also a common theme for him, to buy people lunch or dinner or gifts out of the goodness and generosity of his heart. Tim showed up after practice with some of his teammates, and Gianni knew a couple of the guys that were with him. Gianni put in a pizza order for the guys, and one of Gianni's coworkers, Stevie, took Gianni aside and asked him, "Hey, is everything cool?" Asking him, "Are these guys bullying you? Are they making you buy pizza?"

Gianni laughed. He said all was cool, and he actually invited them. Then Stevie said, "Okay, but I don't trust that little guy. He has beady eyes."

Gianni cracked up and said, "You mean Tim? He is actually the one I am closest friends with." And they laughed loudly. The wrestling team was getting ready to head out, and they walked over to thank Gianni for the pizza. The captain of the team said, "Dude, we want you to know that if you ever need anything, we want to let you know that we got your back!"

Gianni said, "Thanks, guys. And I appreciate the offer. And I got your backs too."

And so from there Gianni had another group of friend—the wrestling team!

The school semester ended, and Gianni would be heading to a new high school in the fall. But for now it was summer break, and it was time for Gianni and his family to vacation in Italy to visit family in the beautiful island of Sicily. It was time for Gianni to get reacquainted with his relatives that he had not seen for about five years—and he got very noticed. His family and cousins were all saying all kinds of things to Gianni, like he had grown up to be a handsome man. And at this point these kinds of compliments were so very embarrassing to him being a modest guy, with him not liking to be the center of attention.

One day a couple of his cousins came over and said, "Let's go over to the piazza for coffee and enjoy the beautiful weather. And our cousin can tell us about America!"

They sat and spoke for a while, and Gianni told his cousins about how life was back home in Chicago. All of a sudden a couple of girls walking in the piazza walked by and began to say good morning to Gianni and kept on walking. His cousins looked at him, and one said, "Hey, cousin, do you know those girls?"

Gianni said, "Nope, never seen them before." And they started laughing and said, "Holy shit." They left the piazza laughing and yet were so very proud of their cousin as they headed back home. They were preparing to head up to their grandfather's mountain farm home for the weekend; most Italians refer to it as Campagna. As they spent the day in Campagna, one of his cousins once again said, "Let's go down to the café and have some coffee." And so they walked down there and had their coffee and then decided to walk over to the piazza, since it was a beautiful evening.

And so they headed over to the piazza, and Gianni decided to get himself a closer look at the fountain and maybe make a wish. And as he stood by, a couple girls were walking toward him, and one of the girls said "Good evening, handsome."

Gianni responded with a good evening of his own, and the girls walked away and began giggling. Of course, his cousins did not miss what had just happened and said, "Oh, Gianni, you know them?"

Gianni just laughed and shook his head no, with his hands together waving back and forth—the *surprised* signal. Once again his cousins laughed, and one said, "Holy shit, cousin."

And he said to them, "This happens to them, right? Girls they never met before will say hello to you?"

They told him, "No, never."

And then one of them asked him, "Why, does this happen to you in America?"

Gianni told his cousins that yes, in America girls he never met before have come up to him and said hello.

He attended a family wedding, and while they were at the restaurant celebrating with food and wine and dancing, his cousins began to go up to Gianni and started telling him that he was getting a lot of attention from the ladies from the bride's side of the family. The ladies were walking up to Gianni's cousins and relatives and inquiring about who he was. That they had never seen him around that side of the family before. And so his cousins were ribbing him a bit about how popular he was with the girls and with their handsome American cousin.

One of them was saying, "You get women who don't know you and say hello to you without you making any effort."

And Gianni then asked his cousins, "What, don't girls just walk up to you and say hello to you?"

It was ironic to Gianni, since this wasn't a new thing for him, to receive attention like this from the girls. So he began getting ribbed by his cousins who had not seen him at the piazza and returned the ribbing to them, and he told them, "Oh this is nothing. You guys should see the attention I get in America. Girls are honking their car horns while I am walking. They come up to me and just start talking to me even though I never met them. They tell me how beautiful I am."

His cousins' jaws dropped, and one was like "Cousin, we need to go to America!"

It is interesting that although he was not back home in Chicago and he was in Italy, he was getting plenty of attention from the Italian girls. A different country, a different setting, and different women. And now that his confidence was getting stronger, his charm or charisma was international. And now he began to think about the song "Breakin'… There's No Stopping Us" by Ollie & Jerry. Many of the words in this song he certainly felt were aligned with some of what he was thinking at that point in time. He felt like nothing was going to stop him now, and soon enough he would start dating a girl that he could say was his girlfriend.

Gianni was returning home from the trip in Italy, and the summer break was about to end. His junior year in his new high school would soon be starting, and Gianni and his family had moved out of the city and into the suburbs. That meant, once again, adjusting to a new school and making new friends. Now he was feeling pretty good about his chances of getting a date after all the attention he got in Italy. And now he had gotten his driver's license and also would be starting a new school. But he also started working a new part-time job for a grocery store near home. There were certainly a lot of new starts for him in the fall: school, job, and now he would have a chance to make new friends at the new school and workplace. The good news for him was that none of the students or his new coworkers he would be associating with and making friends with had any clue about his past, with his lack of experience with girls.

As most people know or can relate to, being a teenager in high school, there were certainly many peer pressures that each faced. Gianni had no interest in experimenting with drugs or smoking. Drinking for him was not a big deal. In Italian culture, you were certainly exposed to some wine or beer. And that culture, or at least in his family, didn't make a big fuss about alcohol in general. His family never sat around drinking heavily and getting drunk. So for Gianni to go to a high school party and drink a beer or two was not a big deal. Nor did he feel the big pressure of needing to drink. And certainly he didn't feel the need to prove anything about drinking. Sex of course not only sells; it is also something that, naturally, people seek and need. And teenagers are no exception to that rule; teenage hormones are certainly running high. The focus for Gianni entering his junior year in high school was to land his first date because he still had not been able to successfully get a date on his own. Although he was an attractive guy, he had to get over the hurdle of being gun-shy to go up to a girl and ask her out on a date. And his blind date that Perry arranged certainly didn't qualify in Gianni's mind as a date.

Gianni transferred to Lincoln High School, a school located in the suburbs of Chicago. Starting his first day of school turned out to be very hectic and particularly strange to him because for the first time since his first year in grade school, he did not know a single person going into the school on the first day. He did what came naturally to him in this kind of situation: stay quiet, observe, and go with the flow! Although this new school was much smaller in size and had fewer students attending, he felt more alone or distant from everyone else at that point. His first class was homeroom class where they took attendance. And then the rest of the day, he would attend his classes on schedule.

The teacher welcomed him to Lincoln, and he had a couple of brief introductions with a couple homeroom classmates. Then he was off to his first class of the day, English. Gianni just was still nervous and continued to stay quiet. The teacher took roll call, and as soon as after Gianni acknowledged that he was present, the teacher immediately asked if he was related to another student that once attended the school a few years earlier. Gianni was positive that he was not related to the person the teacher was referring to, since he knew all his relatives and was positive that none attended this school. The next period for Gianni was a scheduled study break in the library, so he sat in during the break to sort his thoughts and prepare to go to his next class, which was Italian. He thought to himself, *Yep this should be a class I get an A.* And then his next class would be gym, one of his favorite classes at school. So far, it was looking like an easy first day for Gianni—or at least for the morning.

Now he was off to gym class, and it was a class combined with the seniors and juniors, so there were a lot of kids in the gym. And again, he still didn't know anyone, so he stayed the course and stayed quiet. The gym teachers began to talk about the curriculum for the semester and what they were expecting from the students and told the students to be ready to run the track in their next class for qualification times. After the teachers made their announcements, they gave the students time on their own, to sit and talk and to mess around a little.

The volleyball nets were set up, and so Gianni decided to just sit on the bleachers. It was almost like he was sitting isolated. No one came too close, and so he just sat there watching the kids tossing the volleyball around. Then all of a sudden a girl came over and tapped him on his shoulders and began to speak to him. She introduced herself and said, "You are new to the school."

Gianni told her the scoop that he, indeed, was new to the school. He was a junior and didn't know a soul. She said she would be happy to be his friend, and Gianni made his first friend in Diana. She said she was Italian also. "I noticed you were sitting by yourself and not talking to anyone or not hanging with any groups. I figured you must be a new kid!"

Next up was lunch. Wow, back-to-back favorites for Gianni, so he decided to use the restroom before grabbing lunch and then heading out for the afternoon classes. He was about to leave the restroom when one of the teachers approached Gianni and said, "Hey, where are you going? Don't you have a class?"

He said, "I have lunch right now."

The teacher demanded to see his ID, which would show the students' schedule to confirm what he was saying. The teacher then said to Gianni, "Well, what are you doing in here? You got only twenty minutes for lunch."

Gianni said, "I had to answer Mother Nature's call!"

The teacher told him, "All right, go on, get moving to the lunchroom."

Gianni learned later that the reason he was getting so much hell from the teacher was many of the slackers would smoke in the restroom, so the teacher was assuming that Gianni was in there smoking rather than being in class. Plus, Gianni was new, so the teacher didn't know who he was. So now Gianni had like ten minutes to eat and get to his next class, world history. He wolfed down a hot dog and headed over to his next class. Then after that, his next couple of classes. He was just trying to get acclimated to his new school. His first day of school was certainly a hectic day. Between learning where he needed to go for classes and figuring out the school culture, it was certainly a challenge to take all that in a day.

A couple days later, when the next scheduled gym class came up and everyone was dressed for class, the teachers took them outside to the track and said, "Okay, for those of you that are new or not, remember you will be running one-and-a-quarter turns around the track. And you need to complete the run. For the boys, under two minutes is your mark, and the girls would need to make it under two thirty."

Gianna laughed and thought, what was the big deal? He was thinking this to himself as he ran up and down the basketball courts and on the football fields and the bases on the baseball field. This would be a cinch! The shot went off, and everyone started running. About a quarter of the track run was completed, and Gianni was still feeling pretty good about his run on the track. All of a sudden, he said, Oh Shit, he might have started too much too fast. He was beginning to lose his steam, and then he realized that he had to slow down a bit, so he could get adjusted. By the time he got the turn completed, he had another quarter to run, but he didn't know if he could even finish the run. He managed to finish the run, though, and heard the teacher yell out his time: two fifteen! Gianni dropped to the grass of the football field to catch his breath. All of a sudden a girl breathing heavily came over to him and said, "Hey, what was your time?" Gianni told her his time and asked why she wanted to know.

She said, "I was right behind you when you crossed. I didn't hear what my time was, but since I was so close to yours…" She then said, "Hey, you are new here. And I think we are in English class together. My name is Alicia, by the way."

Gianni said, "Yeah, nice to meet you." And he thought to himself, *She's a pretty nice-looking girl. Wow, these girls are pretty friendly here at Lincoln High.*

A few months after Gianni started at Lincoln High, he became friends with Johnny, one of his classmates he started getting chummy with. They decided to hang out at the mall after school, maybe hang out at the arcade for a little while, which was cool with Gianni. They were walking along the mall when Johnny noticed that one of their classmates, Reuben, was walking along with a girl by his side. So Johnny said, "Come on, let's go say hi to him and give him some shit."

Johnny and Gianni approached Reuben. But before they could say hello to Reuben, all of a sudden Reuben's girlfriend screamed out real loudly, "GIANNI!"

Johnny and Reuben both stared at Gianni as he was surprised as they were that she knew who he was, and she proceeded to say, "Don't you recognize me? It's Angela."

And Gianni responded with "I'm sorry, but in this neighborhood there are a lot of girls I know named Angela."

And she then said, "Angela Brucetta, we went to Jacques School together. I was friends with your sister, and we were practically neighbors!

Gianni was like "Oh Angela Brucetta. Yeah, now I remember you. Sorry I didn't recognize you. You don't look like how you did back in the day."

"Oh yeah I know. I changed my hair color and all."

Gianni was like "Hey it was nice seeing you again. But hey, we got to get going. See you at school, Reuben."

They walked away and headed home, and Johnny said to Gianni, "What the hell was that all about?"

Gianni was like "What do you mean? Didn't you hear her? She was friends with my sister, and we went to Jacques School together."

Johnny was like "*Dude*, the way she was practically drooling at you when she saw you."

Gianni responded by saying, "What are you talking about? No way, dude. You are exaggerating."

And Johnny said, "Oh yeah? Wait until tomorrow and you see Reuben. I bet you he will be pissed."

And Gianni said, "But I didn't do anything. Why should he be pissed?"

And then Johnny said, "Noo, not pissed for what you did. Just pissed at you. Wait, you will see."

The next day at school, Gianni and Johnny ran into Reuben in the gym locker room, and Johnny started the conversation by saying, "Hey, man. What's happening, Reuben?"

And then Reuben said, "You want to know what's happening? I'll tell you what's happening. Last night I broke up with Angela!"

Johnny said, "What? Why? What happened?"

Reuben said, "He happened!" He looked at Gianni.

Gianni said, "What? What do you mean?"

Reuben said, "After you two left the mall, she was going on and on about Gianni and his sister and how close they used to be. And how they grew up together. And then she asked me if I could do her a favor and get Gianni's phone number, so she could call up his sister. I knew that was bullshit, and she just wanted Gianni's number!"

Johnny said, "Dude, I'm sorry. It was all my fault. After all, I saw you and I told Gianni, "Hey, let's go over and give Reuben some shit. But I had no idea that it would turn out how it did."

Gianni said he was sorry about what happened. "But maybe it will work out for you two somehow."

Reuben then said, "No, dude, don't worry. I got two other girl-friends I am dating at the same time. So now I will just focus on those two."

Gianni then asked, "You are dating three girls at the same time?"

Reuben said, "Yeah, man, I got to spread myself around."

Johnny looked at Gianni as they changed for gym class. Then Reuben walked out of the locker room. Johnny said, "Hey, Gianni, you buy that story?"

Gianni said, "Oh I don't know. I think he knows two other girls besides Angela. But I don't think he is actually dating all three. I bet he goes from one girl to another. After one doesn't work out, he goes to the next girl. And when that is over, he moves on to the next one. I bet you he has a go-to-next list."

Johnny agreed that he took the breakup the previous day very. "Well, almost too well. But I think he wants an image out there that he is a ladies' man."

By the end of the junior year, Gianni had built up some friend-ships with a few different other junior classmates and found groups to associate or hang out with during the school semester. A couple of his new friends that he found himself hanging around with the most were Johnny and also Tommy. They were hanging out during lunch breaks, and after school they began hanging out, and then par for the course Friday and Saturday nights. They also hung out during the day on weekends.

The semester ended, and Gianni did not get a date with a girl from school or at his new job, so he had to continue to try and find someone to ask out. Tommy liked to go to the flea market on Sunday mornings, and Tommy suggested the three of them go to the flea market, so they might find some deals on some items. So they walked around the flea market, and Gianni got his first experience at a flea market and was very fascinated with the setup of the flea market. Although he didn't make any purchases, he and his friends were having a good time. And when they were done at the flea market it was about lunchtime, so they decided to stop at a McDonald's on the route home.

As they were finishing up their conversation about their trip to the flea market, they decided it was about time to head back home. The boys got up and began to toss out their garbage from their trays, and Gianni was last of the three to toss out his garbage. And as he was tossing out his garbage, there were a couple teenage girls that were sitting nearby, when all of a sudden one of them yells out to Gianni.

"Excuse me! Excuse me!"

Gianni looked up and looked over to them, and one of the girls said to him, "Can we ask what your ethnic background is?"

Of course, Gianni was not expecting that, but he responded by saying, "I am Italian!"

And the girls responded with "Yeah that's what we thought, we think you're *hot*!"

Oh my god, Gianni could not believe his ears. Now he was getting the ultimate compliment, from cute to *hot*! And he responded to the girls by saying, "Thanks!" And he walked away to head over toward his friends with a big-ass grin on his face. Tommy and Johnny started asking Gianni what was that all about and as they walked outside heading toward the car, he began to tell them what the girls had said to him, and the guys said, *What*? "Wow, dude, the chicks dig you," Tommy said to Johnny. "Did you ever have a girl call you out like that in public?"

Both said never had that happen to them, so as they were pulling away, Tommy continued to be in awe of his new friend Gianni and then proceeded to ask Gianni, "So you got their names and phone numbers right?"

And Gianni was like "Yeah. Wait, what? Their names and phone numbers? So you can call them to go out?"

Gianni just put his head down, and both the other guys began laughing and said, "Oh my god, you were practically being served on a platter, and you completely dropped the ball! You did not even have to approach or ask them. They came to you!"

Tommy told Johnny, "Dude we can pick up girls, if Gianni is with us. The girls will just flock over to us!"

Gianni laughed, but he was starting to feel the shell was slowly breaking and now for the summer days ahead and then heading into senior year!

Senior year began, and he was feeling very good about his odds of finally getting a girl to go out with him on a date. He found himself in his Italian class one morning as a senior. He was sitting in class when all of a sudden a couple of freshmen girls from another time slot interrupted to say they had a problem with their field trip and didn't know what to do. Gianni didn't know who they were, except that they were from the freshman class, and the teacher told them there was nothing she could do for them at this time, since she was in the middle of the class and told them to pull up a couple chairs until the class was over, and she would handle it then.

The girls just happened to sit right behind Gianni, and he continued to pay attention to the teacher. When all of a sudden he felt something on the back of his hair down his neck. He swiped it, thinking maybe it was a fly or something. But then he felt it again and this time he turned around, and one of the girls, Marissa, was taking her finger and twirling around one of Giannis's locks. He had wavy hair, so toward the bottom of his hair it would curl up naturally. But he was like "What in the world is going on?" A complete stranger, someone he had never seen, was being aggressive and was flirting with him!

He was a little embarrassed because he was a senior, and here was this freshman messing with him like that. She was not done with her aggressiveness toward Gianni. Every time she passed by him she made a big point to get right in front of him and say hi to him. He would be kind and say hi back but move on and never thought twice about it. So one time one of Giannis's friends, Tony, asked what was up with that. And he replied, "Oh some girl that is not in any of my classes, she seems to have a thing for me."

Tony laughed out; it was funny to him that Gianni was annoyed by this infatuation, and that he was focused on trying to get the attention of other girls in school. Not only was Marissa flirting with him, but Terri his new neighbor that moved in a couple houses over the summer was also flirting with him, saying hi to him when she saw him in the hallways. Once he was coming out of restroom, and she and her friend were walking past it. As he was exiting, she said to him, "Oooh, you were smoking."

He responded with "That's not possible, I don't smoke!"

He thought his senior year was going to be good, and he would get a date, but he had no idea the freshmen girls would be hitting on him.

Late October of the school year, the kids were given a half day of school, so they had the afternoon to themselves. Gianni wanted to see if Tony wanted to hang out. He went up to Tony's locker after class and school was over to ask him if he was going to the mall and if he wanted to hang out. Tony said, "Oh I think I got plans with my new girlfriend Gina, but we need to walk over with to her locker and find out for sure."

As they were walking over toward Gina's and started getting closer to her locker, who did Gianni see standing next to Gina but none other than Marissa? The same two girls that sat behind him that one day in Italian class. He did not know this was the Gina that Tony started dating, and Gianni was like feeling it was an "oh shit" moment. Tony said, "Hey, Gina, are we going to the mall?"

"Oh well, let me see if Marissa wants to come along." She had this big smirk on her face and said very loudly "Oh I will go but only if he goes!" while taking her fingers and grabbing his collar on his shirt and Tony looked over to Gianni and said, "Well, you coming?"

Gianni nodded yes; he felt he did not have a choice but to go with them and did not want to ruin the plans because of his refusal. They went to the mall and grabbed a bite to eat, and as they sat and ate, all Gianni could think about was that he was wishing this would end sooner than later. And although Marissa was interested in Gianni and wasn't shy about letting that be known, and as often as Marissa flirted with Gianni, he was never interested in her. He just was not interested in her that way; he wasn't sure why that was, but he just knew he didn't.

One morning in homeroom class, toward the end of the school year, after school yearbooks were distributed to the student body, Gianni was sitting and conversing with a couple of classmates. All of a sudden Gina walked into homeroom and yelled, "Gianni, there he is the hottest senior at Lincoln!"

All of a sudden that got everyone's attention and were, like, where did that come from or what was going on? Gianni was surprised to also hear that, and Gina proceeded to say that her mom was checking out the class yearbook and saw Gianni's photo and said to her, "He is the hottest boy in the senior class!" Gianni did not know how to respond to this compliment but to say, "Well, Gina, your mom has got great judgment."

After roll call, Tommy went up to Gianni and said, "Man, dude, you even make an impression on the parents!"

Gianni said, "Well, that is good because when I meet the parents of a girlfriend, I want to make a good first impression!"

A few weeks later, and prom was on the horizon. Gianni was feeling the pressure of not only getting a date for the prom but to finally break out of his shell, to actually ask a girl out. He decided it was time to ask someone, and he decided to ask Gina since she told everyone he was the hottest boy in the class, and they were on friendly terms and figured it won't be so difficult to ask. But unfortunately for Gianni he waited a little too long to ask because she had already been asked by someone else in class and had agreed to go with him. It took a lot of courage to build for Gianni to get the nerve to ask a girl out, but now he got that out of his way, and maybe the next time he'd ask a girl out he would feel more comfortable. He did not bother to ask any other girls to prom because he decided to not go to his prom.

CHAPTER 3

The summer before his first college semester was definitely hot for Gianni, and not just because of the summer weather. He was working his part-time job, and then one day a new crew of part-time baggers started working. An opportunity for Gianni to make additional friends outside of school opened, plus they hired a new girl, and her name was Denise. He was instantly head over heels for her. He thought this could be his first girl he'd finally get a date with, and maybe even a long-term girlfriend. He thought she was just right: looks, figure, and personality. It was the perfect girl for him, he thought! He started his move by starting with small talk with her, getting to know her, and hoping to build up the nerve to ask her out!

Finally, he figured out his schedule and her schedule, and when they would be working the same shift, and finally that day would arrive. It was a Saturday afternoon, and he started his shift an hour or so before her shift ended. And he figured he would have cart duty at the hour. As he typically would on a busy Saturday afternoon, he would be outside gathering shopping carts, but then he would time it that he would be walking with her as she headed to her car. But he wasn't alone out there. He had cart duty with his buddy Oliver. He coordinated with Oliver so that Gianni only would be outside while Oliver was inside bringing in the shopping carts, so as the two of them walked together to her car to say goodbye for the day (in his mind he could hear the song in his head by Kool & the Gang— "Tonight"—to help him break his nerve). Gianni finally popped the question and asked her if she would like to go out sometime? (His heart was pounding and racing; he was so nervous.) And she responded with *sure*!

They agreed to discuss the details the next time they were working, and Gianni was so happy he was ready to start jumping up and down in excitement. But he kept his cool until she left the parking lot! Finally she was clear from his site. Gianni began to celebrate his first date by pumping his fist, and Oliver had come back from bringing the shopping carts inside and said, "So it went well, huh? I could see your big-ass grin from all the way inside the store!" He told Oliver he was a little numb; he was a little surprised she said yes but glad she did! Oliver and Gianni had met at Belmont High School, so they knew each other before they began working together.

A couple days later, when Gianni saw Denise and once again she was walking toward her car after finishing her shift, he walked beside her, and before he could say anything to her about when they were going out together on their date, she said, "Listen I can't go out with you. I have a boyfriend and he is 6'2" and 250 pounds!" She said, "I did not want to be rude, so I said yes, but I do not want to keep you hanging around about when we would go out."

Gianni was heartbroken by this news from her. Going from being on cloud nine to hitting rock bottom, he kept thinking to himself, something wasn't right with the picture she just painted. Why wouldn't she initially just have said something to the effect of "Gianni, I would love to go out with you, but I have a boyfriend"? That at least would have had made more sense to him. Oliver came back outside and asked what was wrong with Gianni; he had never seen him like that before. He looked like he had seen a ghost or something. He went ahead and told Oliver the news that Denise told him, and Oliver responded with "No way, dude, she is lying to you. She doesn't have a boyfriend. She had a change of heart or maybe got another offer from someone else!"

He said, "Yeah, I was not buying the 6'2" and 250 pounds bit. She could have told me that right off the bat."

After a couple days passed when Denise gave him the news, Gianni was at another corner of the parking lot gathering carts when he looked up and saw Denise. And there he saw her giving someone a hug and a goodbye kiss. And sure enough the character wasn't the beast she described but simply one of the other baggers from the store! (Now Gianni could hear in his head the song "Misled" from Kool & the Gang.) Oliver came over to Gianni, and Gianni told Oliver that he had seen Denise but had seen her with her new boyfriend, and it was not the football player she was telling him and that it was actually Tim. Gianni went home after his shift and lay down on his bed, and he broke down and began tearing up and had music playing in the background. The song that started playing on the radio was "Games People Play" by The Alan Parsons Project. What perfect lyrics; he felt Denise was playing games with him.

Gianni decided to move on from Denise and called up Johnny and asked him if wanted to play some basketball. After playing a couple of games of hoops with Johnny, they headed over back to Johnny's house, and he began to ask Gianni for his opinion about a girl he knew and on how he should go about asking this girl out that he had his eye on. And since Gianni was so popular with the girls, he might be able to give him some pointers. Gianni thought that was rather ironic that someone needed help with girls would ask him since he hadn't even been successful yet himself. But then he began with asking Johnny some basic questions like who was it and how did he know her. Johnny said it was a coworker of his, and he had begun to make small talk with her but that she had a boyfriend, and maybe she would reject anything more than friendship with him. Johnny had borrowed a high school yearbook from a friend that happened to go to the same school that this girl he had an interest in. Her name was Danica, and Gianni said to Johnny that she was very attractive; she looked like a typical Italian gal in the hood. A few days later Johnny told Gianni that he was speaking to Danica, and he was telling her about what Gianni had said about how she looked like the typical Italian gal. And well, she was not too happy about what Gianni said. At first he thought Johnny was pulling his leg. Why would someone get upset about what he said? It wasn't an insult to her. Nor did he understand why Johnny had mentioned what he had said about her or brought up Gianni in a conversation or how this would even come about in their conversation.

Gianni had not only noticed that he got attention from the girls but that the boyfriends who were with their girlfriends were noticing or checking out Gianni and that he was making them jealous. One such occasion happened a few days after Johnny told Gianni that Danica was upset from his comment about her, and he was working at the grocery store bagging groceries for the customers, when he looked up and noticed a girl in line. Lo and behold there she was—it was Danica! He could not believe it—she was in his line, and she was not alone. In fact, she was with her boyfriend. Gianni had figured this was it. Here she was to give him a piece of her mind, but then Gianni thought, but she never met him before, and how would she even know it was him? But then he realized he had a name tag on his uniform, or Johnny showed her their school yearbook! Gianni decided to switch over to the next checkout line to bag other customer groceries to get away, because he did not want to make it noticeable that he was checking out Danica, nor did he want her boyfriend to notice it and then get into a confrontation!

As Gianni was bagging groceries at the other checkout line, he could see out of the corner of his eye, Danica and her boyfriend walking toward the exit but yet stopped. Gianni could see that Danica was holding back her boyfriend and trying to get him to go to the exit doors and not go over toward Gianni to confront him. Gianni could see them pointing toward him. It looked like her boyfriend was asking Danica, "Do you know that guy?" Or "Why were you checking him out? Why was he checking you out? You guys know each other?" And it looked like Danica responded to her boyfriend with saying no to him and by pulling him toward the exit and looking like she was saying, "Let's go." They finally exited without damage, but Gianni knew he just missed a big confrontation.

A few minutes after Danica and her boyfriend left the store, it was time to rotate from bagging groceries to the parking lot and gathering up the shopping carts. Roger was already out there gathering carts, and when Gianni went over to team up with Roger, he began to tell him that he just missed out on seeing an "almost confrontation" with himself and some jealous boyfriend. Roger was surprised and asked Gianni what he did to stir this, and Gianni went on to tell him it was totally innocent on his part. He told Roger that his buddy Johnny was interested in this girl he worked with, and he began to ask him how he should go about asking this girl out because he really liked her. And so he showed him a picture of her, and he told him she was a typical Italian-looking girl from the hood. And for some reason he turned around and told her that as if it was meant to be an insult to her.

"He then tells me that he mentioned to Danica what I had said about her and that she was pissed and was going to say something to me."

Roger then said, "Why the hell did he tell her that?"

Gianni responded with "I have no idea, he told her where I work, my name. He showed her my photo from our yearbook. There I was bagging groceries, and who do I see in line? Yep, not only her, but her boyfriend to boot. I did not realize it at first, that it was her, but once she got closer to getting her items scanned I realized it was her. I could see she was looking at me, recognizing it was me, but her boyfriend also noticed she was checking me out and I was checking her out. But not for the reasons he was thinking, and I could tell he was getting steamed about this. And so I moved to another register to bag groceries and pretended I wasn't checking her out. But I could see her holding him back by the exit doors and looking over toward me."

Roger laughed and said, "Well, my friend, how do you like being a pretty boy? Not only do you have women who throw themselves at you, but you also have jealous boyfriends who want to throw punches at you!"

As they were talking, Sam had just begun his shift and got shopping cart duty, and so now it was the three of them, and Sam was like "Hey, what's going on?"

And Roger proceeded to tell him about Gianni's near miss of a beating, and Sam began laughing. "You know here I am thinking you got it so easy, but maybe there is another little layer that I never even thought twice about."

Gianni responded to the guys by telling them he was tired about talking about this, but he knew this has yet to be resolved since he needed to confront Johnny and tell him he needed to keep him out of Johnny's business.

After speaking with Johnny and asking him to explain to Danica that it was just a misunderstanding, Gianni was hoping that the Danica ordeal would be over and that he could move on and focus on things related to Gianni and not to Johnny's little mess of pot that was boiling hot and hoping this little ordeal was past him. A couple days after this "almost confrontation" at the store Gianni and Cooper, one of his buddies and coworker, were retrieving shopping carts, and he was mentioning about how Johnny had a thing for a girl and how he got caught up in the middle of her being pissed at him and how she was going to give him a piece of his mind!

Cooper could not believe it also, thought it was strange how Gianni could get dragged into a controversy without being involved! As they were outside retrieving the carts, Gianni could see down the block a couple girls walking and approaching where he and Cooper were gathering the carts. All of a sudden, Gianni realized that one of the girls looked like Danica, and he once again put his head down to look like he was not looking at them or paying attention, when all of a sudden Danica walked right up to Gianni and said, "Excuse me, are you Johnny's friend Gianni?"

Gianni replied back to her yes, and she said, "That's what I thought. I am Danica Santini, and he told me what you had said about me. I want to know why you would say something like that about me, you don't even know me."

Gianni said, it was a complete misunderstanding. "I don't know anything about you, never met you, and I sure would not say anything bad about you. I did tell Johnny that you were very attractive and you looked like a typical Italian gal, but I was only speaking about your looks and not sure how that could be misinterpreted in any way. I never said what type of girl I thought you are because I don't know you to begin to even tell him any such information, so anything he said to you that I said was a complete misunderstanding, and I am sorry."

She said she was sorry also for saying anything and that it was all Johnny's fault that this was blown out of proportion. She then proceeded to say if she could make it up to Gianni by going out sometime? Gianni did not see that coming, but declined her offer since she had a boyfriend and saw how he reacted to seeing him the other day.

She was like "Well, that is okay." She said that she was done with him and his jealous streak, but then Gianni said, "I still can't say yes to going out with you" since Johnny was smitten with her, and he could not do that to a friend, and she should go out with him. She said, "No way, Johnny was a nice guy but definitely not my cup of tea."

Gianni said, "I am sorry" and wished they could had met under better circumstances, and they both wished each other good luck. After the girls left, Cooper was in awe. He said, "Gianni, what the hell just happened? She came over to give you a piece of her mind and then practically begged to go out with you?"

Gianni was like, "Yeah, I don't understand it either. But I know if said yes to going out with her that it would have opened up a big can of worms and I am not going to get involved in such a web" He said, "Look how much trouble there already has been, and I never even spoke a word to her before tonight!"

Gianni could not believe how rumors could get someone into so much trouble and began to hear in the song playing in his head "Rumors" by Timex Social Club.

A couple days later Gianni ran into Johnny and Tommy, and then Gianni proceeded to tell Johnny that he spoke with Danica the other day, and he thought it has been straightened out with her. Johnny began to berate Gianni and was telling him it was all his fault that this thing blew up like it did. If he didn't say she looked like a typical Italian girl he would never had said it to her. Gianni said, "What are you talking about? I thought that it was just the two of us talking. I had no clue you were going to go back to her and tell her every word I said that night."

Tommy said, "Oh okay, it sounds like a misunderstanding, and we can move on forward."

Gianni replied with "That is fine by me."

Then Johnny took a shot at Gianni by saying, "Some friend you turned out to be. I tell you that I like her, and then the first chance you get you ask her out!"

Gianni was shocked and asked "What? What are you talking about?"

"Yeah, Danica told me how when she ran into you, how you were talking bad about me, and then you asked her out, you backstabber!"

Gianni could not believe his ears, Tommy also worked at the store with Gianni and said to Tommy, "You can confirm with Cooper. He was right next to me when Danica came to confront me. This so-called backstabber was trying to calm Danica down to tell her it was just a misunderstanding and what I had said about her looking like a typical Italian girl was not meant as insult at all. When she realized I was being sincere, she then proceeded to apologize to me for the big blowup, and she shouldn't have gone into the store with her jealous boyfriend. And she wanted to make it up to me somehow by offering to taking me out, and I said no thanks, it is okay, you don't need to make it up to me. And then her told her Johnny was a good friend, and he could not do that to a friend." Gianni then told him that he put in a good word in for him. "But call me a backstabber when the whole time she is playing you like a Stradivarius. She is just trying to distract you and make you focus on me so you would be pissed at me and not her."

The friendship between these three friends that started in high school had reached the boiling point and would soon be over a few months later.

A couple weeks after his confrontation on a late summer afternoon while working on his shift, Gianni was retrieving shopping carts with Roger and Sam when former classmate Chuck of Lincoln High pulled in to talk with the guys, and the four of them were talking about possibly attending a big party over the weekend but had to figure out who they needed to contact to know where the party was being held and to get invited or crash it.

It was going to be the best party because summer was coming to a close, and a lot of the people would be attending the party, and many of the attendees would be going away from home to attend college. And then all of a sudden a couple of attractive blond girls pulled up near where Chuck was parked, and the four guys looked at each other in awe from the beauty of these girls. And so Roger and Sam decided they were going to make their move on them. And Roger said, "Excuse me, but don't we know you?"

The girls looked at Roger and Sam and one said, "No, we never seen you before, we have no idea who you are."

And then they looked up and noticed Gianni and walked over to him and then one said, "But we know you, we recognize you. We seen you here many times that we shopped here." And then she suggested they come over to this party they were having on Saturday. They gave him the address and then one said, "See you Saturday" and walked in toward the store. The guys turned to Gianni, and they practically simultaneously started screaming. "Are you fucking kidding?" One of them asked Gianni, "Hey, what are those girls' names?"

"Hell if I know."

"You don't know their names, and yet we just got invited to their party. And not just any party but the party of the summer we been hearing about. This is unreal?" They didn't even want to talk to Roger and Sam, but boy they could not wait to speak with Gianni. While this conversation was going on, Gianni began to hear the song "Take It While It's Hot" by Sweet Sensation and thought he was hot and on fire. The legend of Gianni continued to grow among his friends.

A couple days before the party, Gianni was outside retrieving shopping carts with Oliver, and it seemed like it would be a quiet, hot summer day, when all of a sudden they heard a woman scream-ing in the parking lot toward Gianni and telling him he needed to come over to her. She was too far for him to see who she was, so at that point she was a complete stranger. He looked over at Oliver, and he said, "Dude, you better go over there. She wants you to go over there."

He had no idea what he was walking into, and as he began to inch closer to where the woman was standing, he began to realize who she was, and he said, "Oh it's you!"

It was Anita, and he got to know her through his days at the pizzeria. She was related to one of the other guys he worked with, and she said to Gianni, "I believe you know Frankie" and pointed to the guy next to her.

He said, "Sure, of course. I introduced the two of you."

Frankie used to work with Gianni at the grocery store. She was like, "Well, we just wanted to give you a hard time since we saw you."

Gianni said, "Well, thanks for giving me a hard time and for saying hi."

She proceeded to give him her cart, so he could take it back with him, and then he said, "And thanks for the cart too!"

He made it back to Oliver, who said, "Who was it?"

He said, "Oh I don't know. I never met her before."

Oliver said, "What? Get out of here, no way!"

Gianni started laughing. "I'm joking. The girl is an old friend, and the guy you probably didn't realize was Frankie, who used to work with us."

Oliver was like "Dude, I seen you get attention out here. I really didn't think you knew her when you walked over there, so I figured here we go again, another jealous boyfriend and he is about to get a beating!"

They both had a good laugh, but Gianni knew that that was not too far-fetched and that someday maybe those near confrontations will turn to an actual one!

At the party, Sam ran into someone who he knew, a girl that was his neighbor, and she suggested he come over one night early next week and do some catching up. She had the place to herself, while her parents were on vacation, but that she would not be alone and would have a friend of hers there. So it would be a good idea for Sam to bring one of his good friends, but he should consider the good friend he asked to join them—it should be Gianni! Sam replied with "Yeah of course, who else would it be?"

And so Sam went up to Gianni and told him he needed a favor from him and to join him and the girls, but Gianni had to promise Sam that he would not make a move on his neighbor, since Sam had his eyes on her.

Gianni replied with "Yeah sure, not a problem. But who is the other girl that will be there?"

Sam replied with "Beats me, but we will find out when we get there."

The guys showed up at the girls' place and to Gianni's and Sam's surprise the other girl turned out to be Penny, a girl they both worked with at the grocery store. She had recently quit, and while Gianni was having a conversation with her, he began to ask her where and why she had left. She said her family moved to another part of the neighborhood, so she couldn't get to work anymore. Before Gianni knew it, they were discussing about him graduating school. She mentioned that she also went to the same school. Didn't he remember seeing her there? Gianni was like, no, he didn't recall seeing her. Gianni happened to have his high school yearbook in his car, and they took a walk over and into his car to check out the yearbook, leaving Sam and Tina alone in the house.

At this point Gianni, did not realize it, but Penny was putting the moves on him and was hinting that she would like to give him her phone number, and so they could get together again. Gianni took her phone number and figured he had to start somewhere, after all the other rejections he had gotten so far in his life, even though he was not the one that initiated the pursuing of Penny. Gianni did call her, and they began to make plans to get together and hang out. After going out on their first date, at the end of the date Gianni and Penny kissed. It was his first kiss with a girl, right on the lips, and it was so strange to him. He had been wanting to do it for so long, and finally the kiss came along, and he was now beginning to think what else would be next. They continued to see each other, and they continued to kiss—much more than just a kiss. They were making out, and of course that was the first time Gianni had made out with a girl. At this point anything that happened between Gianni and Penny would be the first time for him.

Although Gianni had just recently begun to start dating Penny casually in the fall of that year, one of his buddies from work, Teddy, was talking about heading out with a couple buddies of his, plus his cousin who was visiting from out of town. He said they were going to go to the roller rink to entertain his cousin. Gianni thought about it and figured, sure why not, he had never really been to a roller rink before and would like to try something different for a change. Plus he didn't have plans for the evening with Penny. While they were at roller rink, Teddy ran into a girl he knew, and after a few minutes of talking with her Teddy came over to the rest of the guys and said, "Guys, change of plans, let's get going." And they asked where were they going; he said he would tell them the details in the car on their way there.

They got in the car, and Teddy told his buddy Jack where to go and then proceeded to tell the guys that the girl he was speaking to back at the roller rink had invited him back to her place because she was alone for the night because her parents were gone for the week-end. Then the guys said okay, great, so they were asking what was it they were going to do there, drink and hang out? He said, "Yeah, you guys can drink, but my main plan is for her to fuck my cousin so that he would no longer be a virgin." And oh, he was also going to be getting some action as well, and the three guys could keep themselves entertained while he and his cousin were doing the deed with her.

Gianni was trapped; he was not the driver, and they were practically there. He did not think they would be too long before he knew it would be time to go back home and end this odd night. They finally arrived, and Teddy went into her bedroom and did his deed as he so liked to call it, while the remaining four were in the living room watching TV, waiting. Teddy came back, told his cousin it was now time for his turn at her, and that it was time he lost his virginity! After his cousin went up there, Teddy proceeded to tell Gianni and Jack and John that she was horny and that she might want to take a turn with all five of them that night! Jack was like "No thanks, man, I have a girlfriend."

And Gianni responded with the same thing, that he had a girl-friend, and he did not need any extra side action. Teddy's cousin was done and heading back to the living room, and he said that she told him to send up the good-looking Italian boy next! Well, Gianni was the only Italian among the five, and he said, "No, thanks." And if John wanted to go up there and take his turn that he should go right on up there.

The following week after the roller-rink night with his friends, Gianni and Penny were out on a date one night. They went to the movies, and after the movie they headed out for a bite to eat, and they were driving around after the meal. She began to tell him a story from the past about a girl from school. Penny then went on to tell Gianni about this girl who was confronted by some of the other girls at school about a rumor going around school about this girl being somewhat easy because she had been giving blow jobs to multiple boys from the school.

Gianni said, "Oh was that girl giving a blow job to one of the boys that was dating one of these girls who confronted her?" It sounded like it. Penny told Gianni that she believed that was the case and that was why the girls confronted her.

Gianni said, "Oh well, that makes sense. Why would any girl be upset about a girl giving a guy a blow job unless of course it was her man that she was dating that was getting the blow job from that other girl?"

Gianni began thinking to himself, *Well, this subject of blow jobs is certainly out of the blue.* He began to wonder if there was more to this story than Penny was telling him. As the evening was coming to a close for Penny and Gianni, they parked in a dark, quiet area like they typically would to kiss, but this time Penny was a little more aggressive and unzipped Gianni's pants and told him all this talk about blow jobs certainly had gotten her in the mood and hope he didn't mind her giving him a blow job. Gianni said he was not going to stop her since she was in the mood, and he would enjoy her being in the mood. He figured that all that talk earlier was indeed a prelude to her giving him a blow job. Maybe all that talk earlier was setting up for what she wanted to do for later and to also put him in the mood.

The following date they had, Penny invited Gianni over to her house for popcorn and a movie on the couch for the evening, and he accepted the invite from her. Gianni was finally breaking out of his shell of inexperience and getting some experience, and he only dated Penny a few weeks. This was, for Gianni, his first dating experience—his first girlfriend—and Penny had been digging Gianni well before they ever started dating. They did not go out nightly; they were seeing each other once or twice a week at that point. And it was a good pace for Gianni to break into the world of having a girlfriend and dating. He showed up and rang the doorbell, and Penny opened the door for Gianni, and he walked in as she guided him to the living room where they would be watching the movie. This was the first time he was inside over at her place, so he was not familiar with her house or family.

She said, "Have a seat, I'll grab the popcorn and soda for us, and then we can start watching the movie."

Gianni was beginning to observe the surroundings and began to notice that it was rather quiet in the house. In his house it was always loud. But hey, maybe other households were different. Penny came back with the drinks and popcorn and sat down next to Gianni, and she started the movie. He couldn't but help notice the top she was wearing—some of her buttons were open and low enough to reveal her cleavage, which was not noticeable when he first walked in and which she hadn't dressed that way before. And she also was wearing a skirt, and then he asked her if there was anyone else home? She said that it was just the two of them for at least until midnight or so; her family was at a party in Naperville, about an hour drive from her house.

Gianni was surprised since she made no mention of them being alone, and then a few minutes into watching the movie she began to touch him, getting closer to each other like snuggling together. Then she grabbed one of his hands and guided it toward her breasts and inside her top. She pushed his hand inside her top as he realized she was not wearing a bra, and then she jumped on him, and they began kissing like they had in the past. But this time she was a little more aggressive than usual, and before he knew it she was unbuttoning her top and began to push her breasts toward Giannis's mouth for him to explore with his mouth. They continued their kissing and fondling of her breasts, and as she began lying on her back she began to push his shoulders and head downward to kiss further down and whispered to him to kiss her lower. And he started kissing her stomach, and then she moaned, "Kiss me lower," as she pushed him further down to her pussy and wanted him to perform oral sex on her!

Penny was pleased by Gianni performing oral sex on her that she insisted on giving him oral sex to return the favor as she said.

Gianni was getting nervous now; he could tell she was very turned on and knew what she had in mind, and it wasn't just oral sex she had in mind. And he thought for sure that her family would return much earlier than midnight, and they would get caught being in the middle of whatever it was that they were doing, and Gianni then suggested they call it a night. He told Penny he was getting a bad feeling about her family returning from the party sooner than they told her, and she said okay, that she understood. And sure enough, about fifteen minutes after Gianni left Penny's house, her family had indeed returned home.

The next day Penny called Gianni to tell him his gut feeling was good because about fifteen minutes after he left, they came home. She asked, how did he know? He said he did not know but that he had this weird feeling all of a sudden, and he was also getting uncomfortable that someone was about to walk through the doors and catch them! Their relationship would only last a few more weeks after that night at her house; they were starting to get more distant between the two, especially with Gianni needing to concentrate on his college work and working hard to pay for school tuition. He didn't have much time for dating at that point, so the relationship eventually tapered off. They never had sexual intercourse, and he was not too upset about it. The crazy feeling he had gotten that night at Penny's he never got over and never got comfortable again around her.

As Gianni's first semester was coming to a close and now his first relationship was also coming to a close, he could now focus on his schoolwork and focus on getting adjusted to college-level work. And also he had to make an adjustment to a big campus full of students. He was trying to figure out how to study and work and figure out his major. On the last day of the first semester, Gianni and Tony were attending the same university, and they decided to take the train home after they completed their finals that last day of the semester. They walked into the train and were discussing how their exams went, when right before the train doors were closing who comes dashing in to beat the doors closing? None other than Giannis's longtime friend Renee from Jacques School! As he noticed her, and he was speaking to Tony, he began to say out loud, "OH MY

GOD, RENEE!" as he walked toward her, and she looked up and said, "GIANNI! Oh my god, it is so great to see you!" And they gave each other a big hug hello, and then Tony walked over to say, "So you guys know each other?"

Gianni was like, "Oh, Tony, this is my friend Renee, we grew up together going to Jacques School together. We have not seen each other since graduation."

"How are you doing?"

They discussed how they were now back in school together again, and what a small world it was and began discussing what schedule they had for next semester and turned out they had one class at the same time, and they were both said that would be great, it would be like the old days in grade school and they could sit together.

Gianni was like, "Of course it will be great. Look forward to being in the same class and sitting next to each other and hanging out."

Renee got off at her stop, and they said goodbye, and they would be seeing each other in class soon. She got off the train, and Gianni had a big smile on his face, and then he looked over to Tony.

Tony then proceeded to grill Gianni and he then asked, "So what's the scoop?"

Gianni said, "What do you mean? What scoop? I told you we are friends."

"Yeah, yeah, I got that much. But what's the real deal with you and her? Did you fuck her?"

Gianni responded to Tony, "I have not seen her since we were thirteen or fourteen, I did not mess around with girls at that age."

Tony responded back with "Really? Well, dude, I think she is pretty hot. And she was looking at you like she wanted to jump your bones, and you looked like you were drooling for her! So you going to fuck her now, right?"

Gianni said, "Come on now, don't say that. After all, she has a boyfriend and probably will be getting married soon. And I don't want any uncomfortable feelings when I am around her. Tony, don't try and push me and try to convince me that I need to ask her out. Because at the end of the day she is a friend and someone I grew up with as kids. And I don't think of her that way. To me she will always be Renee from Jacques School. I have never liked her more than as a friend, and it will never go beyond that."

Tony said, "Dude, I don't buy it. Not for a minute do I buy it. I think you have a thing for her and want to bang her!"

"Tony, I don't know how else to say it to you, but yes I do like her. And yes, I think she is attractive. And yes, I had a schoolboy crush on her back in the day. But so did the rest of the boys in class. And there is one drawback to her, and why I am pretty sure I will won't pursue her. She smokes, and that to me is a big turnoff."

Tony reacted. "Ah okay, well, why didn't you say so in the first place!"

Gianni said, "I didn't think I needed to give you a full confession before you dropped it!" The new semester started, and sure enough Renee was sitting in class with a seat waiting for Gianni to sit next to her. And they talked like they had not missed a beat from all those years apart. She was still the same sweet and nice Renee he recalled back in grade school, always a pleasure to talk with her. They took the train home together on the days the class met, and he confirmed some stuff about her—he saw a pack of cigarettes hanging through her purse. She also spoke about her boyfriend, and so Gianni was disappointed to find out what he knew already but was still holding out hope for a different outcome. The semester progressed, and Gianni was struggling with adjusting to college his freshman year. And then he took a break from school, and he never saw Renee or heard from her again. They did not exchange numbers to stay in contact.

Gianni was popular with his coworkers and customers. He managed to win a customer award from a secret shopper that felt Gianni went above and beyond his duties as a deli clerk. When Gianni was asked after about what his secret was to winning his award by coworkers, he simply replied with "I just treat every customer the same and feel every customer should get my 100 percent effort and attention to their needs."

One such example was one night with an elderly pair of ladies. He was taking care of their orders, and as he was getting their order in place, Gianni smiled and said if there was anything else he could get for them. He talked and treated them exactly as he would younger ladies. The ladies responded with no, that was all they needed, but they had to say they were so honored to be served by such a handsome man! Gianni was surprised but managed to thank them for the compliment, and he told them that he hoped they would have a nice night. Well, Gianni was not alone at the deli counter when one of his coworkers said. "Gianni, you not only win awards for great customer service by secret shoppers, but you also get shoppers to compliment you right in front of your face."

When Gianni was not busy getting rewards or compliments from customers or secret shoppers, he kept himself busy hanging out with friends from high school or his friends from the grocery store. It seemed that every weekend there was a party going on during his freshman year. By this time his close friends had been in awe by the fact that girls seemed to just not only steer over to him but that it happened on a constant basis to him, and they were very attractive girls. When there was no party going on, Gianni would go to a poker game to play with his friends. He certainly kept his social life very busy: school chums, work friends, and meeting people from school. It was beginning to really gel for Gianni; his life was so much different from just two summers before when he was working at the pizzeria where he found himself working every Friday and Saturday night. working until 2:00 a.m. and sometimes as late as 3:00 a.m. Although it kept him out of getting into trouble, it certainly didn't do any wonders for his social life. He had finally dated a girl and started getting a little experience under his belt. Time certainly flies by pretty quickly sometimes. And although he did have this little experience under his belt and he was fairly close to getting to his first full sexual experience, he thought about the song "Tonight" by Kool & the Gang. In this case wondering as to when will "tonight be the night he will see the light." He of course was hoping sooner rather than later and hoped a new girlfriend was on the horizon for him.

By the spring of the second year in college, Gianni had gotten a call from his friend Tony, and he said he started dating a girl, and she had a friend and that he should meet her. Gianni was hesitant and reminded him about that blind date he had set up with him a few months back that didn't go so well, and he had other previous blind dates from other friends that also went bad. Tony told him that the last blind date was not planned, and his girlfriend was busy with her girlfriend, and the only way he would see her that night was if he could get another guy to tag along for her friend. That was why it was such a disaster. Gianni then told him, "Wow, that is the same story I got from my friend Perry when he set me up on a blind date. This must be some common thing with girls."

Tony told him he needed not worry about those other dates and promised this should be a big improvement from the date he set him up with last time.

Gianni said, "Are you sure this is not a last-ditch effort, and she needs someone to find her dates?"

Gianni reluctantly agreed to meet this girl blindly despite his bad luck in previous blind dates. Gianni said he was sort of free Saturday night because Roger and Sam and Chuck were hosting a hotel party, but he was sure they would not oppose Tony and the girls also joining the party. Gianni figured that this would be a good setting—in case things were bad, this would be a good way to ease out of a bad situation or step away when things were going bad.

The night before his blind date that Tony arranged, Gianni was working at the store, when one of his coworkers, Hans, was looking into getting a poker game set up for after work and had asked Gianni if he would be interested in joining in the game. Hans told him it would only be a small gathering of four or five guys and would only be a couple hours and small stakes. Gianni told Hans that since he was working until about ten and he did not have any plans for the night, it sounded like a good idea to kill a couple hours. Hans and the other guys were also finishing up at ten, so it was a perfect setup for them. When Gianni got there, it turned out exactly as Hans said it would—just a small group of guys from the store and two girls. One of the girls was his sister, and the other was a girlfriend of hers.

While the evening of card playing progressed, Gianni could not help but notice in the corner of his eye the girlfriend of Hans's sister seeming to be checking him out. But he could not be sure since he was there to play cards, and he was not conceited to think every woman checks him out. Plus, he did not find her to his liking and did not find her attractive. And he was not checking her out, and so he did not give the eyeing from this girl a second thought. They continued playing cards, and Gianni was not even thinking about the blind date he had tomorrow and figured it was probably going to be a wasted evening with this girl, and he was glad that the guys had a party planned because he was not even looking forward to this blind date. A couple hours passed, and no one lost a ton of money, and they decided to call it a night. The evening was over, and he was heading home to get some much-needed rest.

Saturday evening arrived, and Tony picked up Gianni, and then they headed over to pick up the girls. He had no idea what she looked like, only by Tony's description, and he knew he couldn't rely on that. Tony told him that he would come back to the car with the girls, and his date would be the tall one of the two girls. Gianni sat in the car, waiting, which seemed to take forever for them to come out to the car. He was starting to think that this was a big mistake, and he was going to regret the decision to come out and meet her. And when they finally came out of the house, to Giannis's surprise he actually found her very attractive and had done a double-take look to see if his eyes were not deceiving him.

The girls sat in the back seat while the guys sat in the front. Her name was Stephanie, and Gianni began speaking about the hotel party that his friends were hosting and began to describe what they could expect to see as far as behavior from the guys at the party. He told them that Roger and Sam and Chuck were very much on cue, and he said they typically acted the same way every party, so he would not expect any less from them tonight. They got to the party, and sure enough as if Gianni had written the script for the girls and Tony, the guys acted exactly as Gianni was telling the girls and Tony during their drive to the party. Gianni took a liking to Stephanie fairly quickly and was very much was interested in seeing her again. And he was hoping she felt the same way and hoped he would see her again, but with his luck so far in his young life, he faced the reality that she may not be interested in him. But for now had to wait to get feedback from Tony after the date was over.

The next day was Sunday, and Gianni was feeling pretty good from his blind date the night before and was anxiously awaiting to hear back from Tony about what Stephanie thought of him. And this was pretty much all he had on his mind all day. As the day turned to evening and he was at work closing up the shop for the night, he saw Hans walk over to him as he was cleaning up some of the equipment for closing the department. And then Hans started the small talk with Gianni and asked him what was up and how it was going and then asked Gianni if he remembered his sister's girlfriend from Friday night's poker game? Gianni responded yeah, he remembered her, why was he asking?

Hans said, "Well, the girls asked me to talk with you and let you know that my sister's girlfriend liked you and was wondering if you would be interested in going out with her?"

Somehow this did not come as a surprise to Gianni since he saw the way she was eyeing him on Friday night. But he was a modest guy, so he didn't want to assume that it was anything more than someone just taking a look. Gianni then told Hans that it was interesting that she was interested, but it just so happened that he met a girl last night at a party, and he was head over heels for her and they hit it off pretty good. And this looked like someone he would be dating for a long time. Hans said he understood and would pass the word on to the girls, and he told Gianni he hoped he understood that it wasn't his idea to ask him but that his sister and her friend were giving him a hard time about approaching him.

Gianni said, "Oh sure." he told Hans he completely understood his situation since he grew up with two sisters himself, so he knew where he was coming from, and it was all cool. Of course, at this point Gianni was still waiting to hear back from Tony if Stephanie indeed wanted to see him again. He was getting anxious since anything that could go wrong for him seemed to go wrong for him. On Monday, finally Gianni got the feedback from Tony, and yes Stephanie wanted to go out again with Gianni. They set up another double date, and after that date Gianni and Stephanie began dating and seeing each other often. And it looked like it might be that girl and relationship he had been seeking. He just had that really good feeling inside him.

After a few weeks of dating, Gianni was feeling very comfortable with her. He was starting to fall in love with someone, and he began to hear the song in his head, "Spring Love" by Stevie B. The words were appropriate, he felt. He met her in the springtime, and he certainly was falling for her. He did not have these feelings when he was around Penny, so he knew this was different. He was not sure why that was the case, but he was enjoying his company with her when they got together.

Gianni wanted Stephanie to feel as if she was a big part of his life, and one way he felt that could be accomplished was by introducing her to some other friends of his and his family and his coworkers. He felt that she would be able to better understand any stories or situations he had told her or would tell her. So off they went to the grocery store where he worked, and there he figured he would introduce her to some friends of his that he was also hanging out with, like George, since she had not met him yet. He also went on to introduce her to his coworkers in the deli department since. That was where he was stationed at that time, and one of the coworkers from the deli he introduced her to was Dana, and she always liked flirting with Gianni. She was older, divorced, and with kids. And well, Gianni was not just regulated to women in his age group, for women to get aggressive with him. Dana managed to say hello to Gianni in her usual friendly way, and when they walked away to go find George and a couple others, Stephanie told Gianni she did not like how she said hello; she seemed a little too friendly and flirty.

Gianni defended Dana and told Stephanie that they were just coworkers and that she was only being friendly. Stephanie still was not happy despite his reassurances. Gianni began to think how glad he was that he never told Stephanie about some of the flirtatious things Dana and him would say to each other back and forth. Many times she would say sexually explicit things to Gianni. Dana was the first woman in his experience that had said sexually explicit things to him. Gianni did not object to it because he actually enjoyed it, made for a better shift at the store, and he did not take it very seriously. But again it was a good thing he did not mention it to Stephanie prior to them meeting because the friendly hello would have definitely been interpreted as meaning more than the friendly greeting that it was. Before Gianni started dating Stephanie, Dana and Gianni would exchange some rather explicit thoughts, and he knew Stephanie would grow even more suspicious if he told her some of the exchanges they had. One example of such an exchange between Dana and Gianni as when they were working, and it was just the two of them. All of a sudden, Dana said, "Hey, Gianni, why do you want to mess around with the young, inexperienced girls?" Gianni asked Dana what she meant by that, and she said, "Well, why would you want a blow job from a girl who practices on a lollipop, when someone like me has practiced on a real cock and knows how to give a blow job!"

Gianni was surprised how blunt she was and began laughing, but then at the same time he was wondering if she was just teasing or if in some way she was hinting to Gianni that she wanted him.

Gianni and Stephanie hung out as often as their schedule would allow them to spend time together, weeknights or weekends. He met her family, and she met his, and people were even suggesting that they were beginning to look like a couple. Much to Giannis's surprise, he continued to get attention from girls even while Stephanie was around him, and he certainly did not try to get this attention. The first such example was one time in the first summer they were together, and so was Tony and his girlfriend, and they had decided to spend the day at the amusement park. Then at one point they were all standing in line, waiting to go on one of the rides, when all of a sudden Stephanie turned to Gianni and said, "If that girl continues to stare at you, I am going to beat the crap out of her!"

Gianni was unaware of any girl staring at him and was confused and asked. "What or who are you talking about?"

Stephanie said, "That little blonde in front of us."

And he said he had no clue, and if she had not pointed this girl out, he would not even have noticed her. He could not believe that someone was showing a little jealousy, and that Stephanie truly had feelings for him to show this little bit of jealousy of someone that may or may not have been looking at him. They finally reach the ride, and who should happen to sit right in the seat right in front of

Gianni? None other than the suspected blonde that Stephanie had been complaining to him about! He knew this could lead to trouble, and he was hoping Stephanie might have calmed down, but when he looked at her, he knew by the look on her face that she was steaming even more! So sure enough, as Gianni was speaking to Stephanie and mentioning about the ride and how wild it was, the girl turned around and had a big smile and spoke to Gianni and agreed with him about the ride. Stephanie almost jumped up, but Gianni had his hand on her leg and pushed down and told her to remain calm and that all was okay, he promised. He tried to assure Stephanie it was not big deal, but he knew that she was right, and the girl was checking him out. He had seen that look on girls many times before.

Stephanie did believe he had eyes only for her as their relationship was building up and they constantly hung out and kissed and touched each other very passionately. And there was an occasion or two when they almost had sex. One day Stephanie told him that her sister was going away for the weekend and asked her to stay at her apartment, keeping an eye on her pets while she was gone, and she told her she could also have Gianni over if she wanted to have company and not be by herself. Stephanie asked Gianni if he would stay with her and keep her company for the weekend and that they could spend time alone together, and he was more than happy to spend time with her. He loved spending time with her and always looked forward to seeing her every chance he had.

At this point in the relationship, they had not engaged in sexual intercourse. And by Gianni's assessment of the situation, the weekend together was not just about caring for the pets. This would be a perfect opportunity for the two of them to share a loving memory of the first time they have sex with each other, and it would be done in a romantic setting, just the two of them. Although Stephanie and Gianni did not actually say the plan for the weekend was to finally have sex, it was understood by both that this in fact was probably what was going to happen. They arrived at the apartment, and they had dinner together on their first night. And then they sat on the couch and began watching television together, like they would normally, but this time Gianni was dressed in more relaxed clothes, sweats, and a T-shirt, while Stephanie had on a one-piece short nightie.

Gianni knew that that was his signal from her that she didn't want to just watch television, and Gianni did not need to worry if he would be pushing her, and they sat closely first cuddling up together, and then they began kissing. They were touching each other until it got too heated for the couch, and they made the slow walk to the bedroom and continued on their passionate kissing and removing of each other's clothes and until they were naked and engaging in having sex. For Gianni, when they started and by the time they finished, it seemed to go very slowly—almost like in slow motion. When he and Penny were getting closer and doing more things, they seemed to go very quickly, but in this case, it was the total opposite.

Stephanie was nervous, since she never had sex before. And well, Gianni did not want her to feel any more nervous and did not mention that this would be his first time as well. And after their first session of sex, they both had big smiles, and both were relieved the pressure was gone. Now they could enjoy sex for the rest of the night as well as for the rest of the weekend. And they certainly did it many times that weekend, trying different positions, even timing how long their sessions lasted and counting how often they did it. It was like a little game for the two of them. It was their little game, and both were very satisfied and happy on how wonderful their weekend was. The thing was that both of them had heard from others about the first time they had sex with someone and how horrible it was or how awkward it was. But for Gianni and Stephanie, it was as natural and loving as a couple could script it to be. Or maybe it was the pace they were going that made the first time so pleasant for them.

Over time, Stephanie noticed the legend of Gianni and girls being aggressive toward him that had started for him since around high school and still going strong. One hot summer afternoon into their second year of dating was no exception. They both decided that they were in the mood for some ice cream, and Gianni and Stephanie drove over to the local ice-cream shop near the home of Gianni. They were the only two in the shop at that point, and she was trying to decide what flavor ice cream she wanted. And so she walked over to the other end of the counter, when all of a sudden Gianni looked up at the door. And who came in but two girls from his high school days? And he knew both well, and one of the girls happened to be Terri his neighbor. Gianni knew her well, and they were not strangers because of being neighbors and going to school together. So as soon as she and her friend saw him, Terri said, "Hi how are you doing?"

Gianni of course responded back by saying hello back and asking how she was doing, when all of a sudden Stephanie was right up next to Gianni and said she was ready to order, and the girls walked over to the other side of the counter. Stephanie then asked, "Who was that?"

And he told her that the taller one was his neighbor, and the other was her friend, and he knew them both from high school. And then Stephanie said, "That is your neighbor?"

And he could see she was in disbelief. And so they both ordered their treats and then sat at a table and so did the girls a few tables away. As they sat down and began to eat their ice cream, Stephanie began to grill Gianni. She was asking him things like "You seem to know them well, and they seem to know you also."

Gianni said yes, he knew both girls. He told her they went to high school, and it was a small school, so everyone knew each other. Then she said. "So why are they are looking at me like that?"

Gianni had no idea and told her he did not know why but could only guess since the girls knew him, and they'd see him with her, that they were probably trying to figure out who she was. If they perhaps knew who she was, etc. The grilling continued when she asked, "So how old are these girls?"

Gianni said he was not sure exactly how old they were, maybe sixteen, maybe seventeen? She responded with "Sixteen or seventeen? Those girls look older than that!"

He responded with "Well, don't most young girls try to make themselves up to look a little bit older than they are?"

They finally left the ice-cream shop, and as Gianni was driving, Stephanie continued to give Gianni a difficult time about the girls and how she was not happy about the girls looking at her that way or the way they were so friendly toward Gianni, smiling and making conversation with him as if they were best of friends.

Gianni replied with "Will you stop making a fuss over a couple girls that I was once classmates with?" He added that she should not feel threatened by them, and then she got upset and said to Gianni, "Pull the car over, pull the car over. Let me out of the car."

Gianni could not believe what she was saying, and so he pulled the car over into a forest-preserve parking lot, and sure enough she got out of the car and started walking away from the car, and then she sat on the cement block of the parking space. So Gianni sat in his car for a minute or so. He needed to gather his thoughts and let Stephanie cool off. Finally, he stepped out of the car and walked over to her and sat down next to her and said, "So did you cool off yet?"

She replied with yeah and began to slap him on his arms and thighs and said, "You did not even come running after me when I walked out of the car!"

Gianni said, "Where were you going to go? You are nowhere close to home or anyone's house but mine!"

She said, "Still, you should have come running after me."

Gianni said, "Look, I am here now. I was not going to leave you, and so I gave you a moment to cool off and collect your thoughts. And hopefully you now realize that the girls were not a big deal."

And she replied with, yeah, she knew better now. "And by the way," she told Gianni, "your neighbor, you are not her type!"

Gianni was not expecting that and responded with "Rightttt..." And he wondered how could she know this girl's type when she didn't know her? But he was not looking for this argument to continue on, so he tried to end it there. Because if he had told Stephanie some of the aggressive things she had showed Gianni when they were in school or when they crossed each other's paths at home or at the mall, it would have just made the situation worse!

One evening, after Gianni spent the day with Stephanie, he told her he would be going to hang out with his friends Roger, Sam, and Chuck and that they would be watching a Chicago Bulls playoff game together. Off he went to meet his friends at the bar near his home. He parked in the first space he could find. The bar was next door to a motel/hotel, and he got out of his car to make his way to the bar to meet his pals, when out of the corner of his eye he could see a woman standing out on the balcony of her hotel room and then suddenly yelled down to Gianni, "HEY!"

Gianni looked up and responded with "How are you doing?"

And she responded to Gianni by saying, "Room 219!"

Gianni's mouth simply dropped and could not believe his ears. He was thinking to himself, did that woman just tell him to come up to her hotel room? Where was this coming from? So he continued on to the bar to meet his friends. And when he got there his friends began to notice that something was not right with Gianni, and they began to ask him what was wrong. "You don't seem yourself."

Gianni said to them, "You will not believe what just happened to me. I don't even it believe it myself, and I was there." And he went on to tell them that this girl told him to go up to her room, told him the room number and all, and the guys replied back with "You got to be fucking kidding us."

He said, "No, guys, no joke. I swear to God this just happened."

And then one of them said, "Well, what the hell you doing here and not up there fucking that girl?"

He told the guys, "Come on, guys, I have a girlfriend. I can't do that to her. Plus, that just seemed too easy. I did not even try to pick her up, and she was inviting me up to her room. No name, no introductions, just a hello? I don't think any of you guys would have gone up there either. But hey, what do I know?"

Sam started saying to the guys, "You know how many times we continue to see women throw themselves at this stud? We all have seen it: parking lot of the store, we seen it at parties. Gianni, dude, what do you do to get this all this attention? Tell us what you do to get this because none of us ever get this attention. We are the ones that try to pick up girls, and you don't even try and the girls flock to you."

Gianni said, "Guys, I honestly do not do anything. You see me, I am quiet, I keep to myself, I smile, and I observe. And before I know it, girls are coming up to me, or twirling my hair, touching my shoulders or chest, coming up to me to say hello."

Chuck said, "Okay, guys, look. If he knew, don't you think he would tell us? First of all, every time we seen these girls throw themselves at him, he is more surprised than we are. And if he is more surprised than us, then he does not know what the answer is either."

Despite all the grief that Stephanie put Gianni through in regards to the attention he would receive and all the other expectations they had set for their future together to one day get married, Gianni really did love her with all his heart. He cared very much about her. This was definitely his first love; they were already together for three years. And Gianni finally got to experience not just love but also a sexual relationship. He actually cared and loved her, and the sex was special for them. They would hang out a lot together, and from time to time their friends would see them and make comments that they looked like one of those yuppie couples. It was humorous to Gianni. That to him showed that their love for each other was noticeable to everyone around them. Through the three-year relationship, they went to the mall looking at possible engagement ring styles she liked. They were talking about how many kids they would have and what names they would pick for them, where they wanted to live, and so forth.

Something happened toward the end of their three-year relationship, and Gianni felt that the beginning of the end was when Stephanie felt she needed to move out of her parents' house and quit going to college and start working full-time. Something else that continued to bother Gianni was the fact that Stephanie kept telling Gianni that she wished he would get his having an affair with another woman out of the way, implying to him that all men did that! Stephanie continued by saying to Gianni that he was too good-looking to be an exception to this rule of men cheating, and it did not matter that he never cheated on her but that he would at some point he would. No matter how many times he tried to assure her there was no reason to feel he would be unfaithful to her and he told her he was disciplined and loved her too much for him to steer in the path of unfaithfulness to her, she wouldn't believe him.

He was not a hypocrite. If he expected his woman to be faithful to him, Then, he should hold the exact same standards for himself as well! At the end no matter how many reassurances he gave or that he promised how faithful he would be to Stephanie, she told Gianni that the fact that she was convinced it would eventually happen that he couldn't stay true to her, and that they needed to move forward and find someone else. Her words were that he needed to find someone better than her. After all the things she was saying, he began to get suspicious of her new boss. It wasn't that Gianni saw anything they did or that she slipped and said something to draw suspicion about him, but it was a deep down gut feeling he got and that he could not shake off that something was not right. He could not believe he was being dumped by the first woman he ever loved and because she suspected he may not be faithful to her despite there being no indications or evidence that his personality or his behavior showed otherwise.

Gianni suspected that there had to be more to this dumping by Stephanie. He just didn't know exactly what it was that was going on for her to just walk away from a relationship that not that long ago there was the talk of marriage and family being discussed. Gianni knew one thing for sure: he could not fix the mess that was now their relationship. He knew it was over, and he would have to move on and find someone to replace Stephanie and live happily and show everyone he was emotionally strong. But when he sat back and thought about the relationship, he began to think about the song "Shattered Dreams" by Johnny Hates Jazz. How he thought they were so dedicated to each other and the all the excuses she was giving him to break it off with him, and then he started thinking his dreams of getting married and having a family were now shattered as if reality had finally hit him.

Gianni was very hurt from the breakup with Stephanie, and he really didn't know what he wanted to do next. After a few months had passed and Gianni was trying to heal, his friends decided to try and get him back on track. First, Will, his buddy from the grocery store, told him about a girl he wanted to introduce to him and thought Gianni should meet her. He told Will he would have to get back to him since he had to check his work and school schedule before he could commit to meeting anyone. He was stalling, really, because he didn't even know if he actually wanted to take the next step and actually go out with another girl at this point in time, and maybe he needed some more time to heal from the wounds. The song "Scars of Love" by TKA certainly fit how he was feeling at that point.

The second thing was that Gianni got a call from his friend Teddy who used to work at the grocery store, and he told him how he had to meet this girl he knew for a date, so now he just received a second offer for dates from two different friends. After he got off the phone with his friend Teddy, he took a very deep breath and let it out somewhat loudly as his supervisor Mitch walked by and asked him if there was anything wrong. He didn't want to show Mitch that he was hurting from the breakup and went into the denial persona and said, "Well, you know how Will, just before he left, said he had a girl he wanted to introduce me to. And now my buddy Teddy called me to tell me he had a girl for me to meet. And now I got two offers to go out with two different girls. And I can't make up my mind which girl I should go out with. Or maybe I should give both a try?"

Mitch looked at him and said, "Say what? You have two potential dates lined up?"

Gianni replied, "Yes, that's the gist of it."

And Mitch said, "You fucker, I never had more than one date ever anytime, and here you are on two-date offers within a half hour of the other!"

Gianni said, "Yeah. Hey, you think I should take one out during the day and the other later in the evening? Or should I do it on separate days?"

Mitch then went on to say, "Oh go fuck yourself, asshole!"

Gianni just began laughing because when he first began to tell him his situation, he really had no idea that Mitch would react that way. And then he realized how it was getting under his skin, and Gianni thought he would have a little fun with it just so that he would continue reacting that way to him! What Mitch did not know was this was the first time Gianni ever had two-date offers at the same time, so this was not something Gianni had going on a regular basis. And if Mitch had known that it was just a few short years ago that Gianni couldn't even get a single date with any woman, he probably would not have reacted the way he did. The two girls he met did not go very well, and nothing developed from it. He just was not mentally or emotionally ready to move on.

CHAPTER 4

Gianni began spending time on the internet in the internet chat rooms and began chatting with girls from the Chicago area. He felt like it was harmless after all they were simply chatting by instant messenger. He was taken aback by how some of the girls were very sexually explicit in some of their conversations. The only woman that spoke explicitly to him was Dana, and that was more done in fun than actual conversation, and he never ever spoke with Stephanie in that manner. So this was definitely new to him. After developing some friendships from the chats and then building a buddy list he developed online, what came next was not what he had not planned on, and that was to meet anyone in person. But he figured he was single and was it any different from striking up a conversation at a bar with a woman over having a conversation with someone online? He felt like he got a better idea of who the woman was or the kind of woman she was over time they chatted online. The only drawback was that he did not know what these girls looked like and was only going by what they had described themselves to him.

The first girl he met was a woman who was a little older than him, and they lived somewhat near each other. Her name was Rose. He knew her age, and her description was tall with dark hair, and he also knew what her ethnicity was. She also mentioned that she was on the curvy side. They picked a bookstore to meet at to sit down and meet for a cup of coffee and have a conversation and see how things went. Gianni was nervous as he could be. He knew the time and the place and what she would be wearing, so they would know who they were when they finally met. He was disappointed because he was not attracted to her. She was much larger than he had anticipated, and the whole time they had coffee together, he was never comfortable.

He could never come up with a good topic to have a conversation with her, and the whole time he kept thinking to himself when this meeting was going to end!

He looked down at his watch, and it had only been five minutes since meeting outside at the bookstore! After their meeting they headed home and then went online and instant messaged each other online to give each other their feedback about how they thought it went. She told him she was totally attracted to Gianni, and he was actually surprised. He thought the conversation was okay but nothing to write home about. And well, Gianni did not want to be rude to her, so he thanked her for the compliments. She began to tell him about what beautiful eyes and smile he had and what a nice body he had, and then she asked him what he thought of her. He knew he could have been rude or nice to her, but since he was not a rude man he went on to tell her how she had a nice smile also, and her eyes were nice. And her top definitely gave him a nice view of her cleavage. She said that she was glad that she made an impression on him and then told him she had to confess something to him.

He told her to go ahead, what was it that she wanted to confess? And she began to tell him after a few minutes of sitting down for coffee that she could not get it off her mind, giving him a blow job—that was how much he turned her on! Gianni thought to himself, well that was certainly direct, and he was not sure what to say to her. She said she hoped she would get the chance of giving him that blow job and that he would be more than welcome to get a much-closer look at her cleavage, along with her nipples! Gianni did not want to be rude and told her he had a busy schedule ahead, but if they both had some free time they should get together again. But since he was not attracted to her, he was not going to make any effort see her again.

The next woman he met from his buddy list was woman around his age, and her name was Gloria. And once again, he only knew what she looked like based on her description, so he really had no idea of what she looked like. It was not a very advanced planned meeting; it so happened one evening that they were chatting, when all of a sudden she suggested they meet. And so he figured, why not? They met at a parking lot, and they both agreed on where they would meet and what time and what kind of car each one had. He was not sure how attractive or unattractive she would be or how accurate of a description she had given him. They both arrived at the designated area of the parking lot, and they came out of their cars, and they stood outside their cars conversing with each other. She was attractive, which made him happy. As they spoke, she began to hint that one of her favorite things to do was kiss and make out, and she repeated it again and again. Gianni understood her hints, but something about her he just was not interested in—messing around with her. So after a while of getting together and talking, they both parted ways and went home. Gianni did not feel good about the meeting. It was probably because meeting someone from the internet in person was just so strange and new to him. This was still very new to him, plus dating after Stephanie was still weighing on him, and so far his first two online meetings did not go well. Or they could have gone better if he was more aggressive or attracted to them. So dating for him was still a difficult transition, and he was not sure how much longer it would be before he would get past the Stephanie relationship.

Another woman Gianni was chatting with online was named Lisa, and they ended up exchanging phone numbers in case they wanted to speak by phone sometime. At least that was what he had in mind. One day, to his surprise, he had gotten voice mail from this girl while he was at work. So he returned her call, and before he knew it, she was wondering if he would like to meet up in person. He was a little surprised since they had not spoken on the phone before. He agreed to meet her even though he had no idea of what she looked like at this point. They decided on what time and where to meet— after work for him and after her night class for her. And they picked a place near where she was going to school. To Gianni's surprise, when they met, Lisa was incredibly attractive! There were so many things that was going through his mind at that moment, and he thought to himself, *Wow, did I get lucky to meet such a beautiful girl.*

They began to chat, and some of the things that were going through his mind he came right out and asked her, "You said you and your husband are separated?"

She responded yes, they were separated but still living together. Gianni was not sure how to react to that because he did not know they were living together, and then he asked why were they separated? She responded with he does not have any interest in her nor were they any longer having sex. At that point Gianni's mouth dropped, as if to say how can any man not want to be interested in her or want to have sex with her? Was he insane? Then she went on to ask him, "So what do you think, want to have sex?"

Gianni responded by saying, "You mean now? But where would we go?"

She said, "We can rent a room at a motel around the corner."

Oh my god, Gianni was thinking in the back of his mind, *what in the world is going on here?* He thought he was meeting a woman for a cup of coffee, but he had no idea he was about to get drawn into a messy situation. He thought to himself, *Wait a minute, is she telling me the truth about the husband?* Was she just cheating on the guy to make him jealous? Was he one of those ragging jealous husbands that follows his wife on her every move and then Gianni ends up on the front pages of the papers the next morning—jealous husband kills wife's lover! Gianni declined the offer and said he had never been involved with a separated woman before and was not comfortable with the situation. He assured her she was attractive, and if she was divorced or single, he would have taken her up on the offer.

The next woman Gianni had been chatting with online was Missy. She was a recently divorced woman, and so Gianni and Missy chatted for a few weeks and then decided to meet in person one evening. They met at a club for drinks and some dancing. And for some reason Gianni was feeling frisky that evening, and it did not help matters when Missy was being flirtatious with Gianni during their evening of dancing and drinking. They decided to leave the club and head elsewhere and got themselves a motel room near the club. This was new to him—he had never met a woman at a club, and all of a sudden found himself in a motel room having sex.

He thought to himself that she was an attractive woman. She had a nice figure, and he never thought he would chat with a woman online and meet her in person and then have sex with her. They had sex for a while, and the whole motion of them having sex seemed to go extremely fast. It was like they walked into the room, and all of a sudden they were naked and having sex. This also was a new experience for him, since all his prior experiences were having multiple dates, then kissing and making out, touching on the next date, and next time something else unlike this night with Missy—they walked in and had sex as if they had many dates prior to meeting that night. They had sex that night until they decided to call it a night and go their separate ways. This was his first sexual experience with a woman outside of Stephanie, and this felt rather strange to Gianni to be with another woman. His feelings were still strong for her, and he needed more time to get over the heartbreak.

As he was driving home after having sex with Missy, he started to feel really awful about having sex with this woman. It was as if he felt like he cheated on Stephanie, even though they were not in a relationship with each other anymore. The next day Gianni went online, and Missy was online, and Gianni began to tell her how he was not over his ex-girlfriend and did not feel right about what they had done last night and did not feel it would be right for them to see each other again because he was not going to get over his ex anytime soon. Gianni was still reeling from the feelings he had for Stephanie, and that was why he felt guilty about having sex with another woman. And the fact was that he needed more time to heal from the wounds. Gianni was struggling after the breakup with Stephanie to find a woman to date, and once again the disappointments were seemingly starting to occur time after time.

Gianni had to get himself back on track to meet someone and have that relationship that he badly wanted. The relationship with Stephanie certainly gave him an inside track of being in a relationship, but he wanted the next relationship that would lead to him getting married. After his initial meetings with the girls that a couple of his friends introduced him to and the girls he met from the internet had not worked for Gianni, one of his good friends from the grocery store, George, was getting married and he had asked Gianni to be one of his groomsmen. At the church Gianni was speaking to some of the other guests, and some of them were from the store that they had worked at, so naturally Gianni would say hi to them. When they were at the banquet hall sitting at the main table for the wedding reception and the reception was getting past the dinner and the dancing was about to start, one of the other groomsmen went up to Gianni at the table and said, "Wasn't that the girl you were talking to at the church?"

Gianni asked, "What girl?"

And he pointed and said, "The girl in the blue dress over there."

Gianni saw the girl he was pointing to and said, "Umm, *no way*, that woman is way hotter than the girl I spoke to at church, definitely a different girl."

The groomsmen began to tease Gianni and said, "Oh well, that is okay. Why don't you go over there and ask her to dance?"

Gianni then said, "Who? Me?"

One of them said, "Yeah, you must. You are the only one single at this table. Everyone else is spoken for, so you got to do it for us. It is your duty!"

Gianni knew he had no choice but to go because he would not hear the end of this until he at least walked over there. So finally he got up and walked over to the table to where the girl was sitting. And as he got closer to her table, he could see her relatives pulling on her arms to join them on the dance floor, and she was refusing to go on the dance floor. Gianni was thinking to himself, *Oh man, that is a bad sign.* But he thought a moment and said, "Fuck it, go over and ask her to dance. If she says no, at least you can go back to the table and tell the guys that she said no to you."

Gianni took a deep breath and then walked over to her and said, "Excuse me, would you like to dance?" And before he could finish his request, she literally jumped out of her chair and said yes! And they walked onto the dance floor, and Gianni was in shock. He was like "Wow, this is so cool."

She said yes. Her name was Laura. George and the rest of the groomsmen noticed that Gianni was on the dance floor with her, and they were like proud brothers, proud that Gianni who recently got out of a relationship was moving on.

The two of them walked over to the bar and grabbed a drink, and Gianni asked if he could call her sometime and she was like "Oh sure." And he was like "Let me get something to write it down." And he turned to the bartender, who just happened to have a pen and paper handy as if he were expecting this to happen. Laura told him that instead of her giving him her number that he should give her his number, and she would call him. Gianni was not sure how to take that if he were getting blown off all of a sudden, but he was not going to argue about that detail. And if she liked him, she would call him. A week after the wedding, George returned from his honeymoon and called up Gianni, and Gianni said, "Oh George, how was your honeymoon? How are you guys doing?"

George responded with "Yeah we are fine, but cut the bullshit. What is the story with you and Laura? You know, the girl you were dancing with all night?"

Gianni then said, "Oh her, yeah, I gave her my number. But I never heard back from her. She must have had a change of heart or something."

George was surprised because he thought that she was available to date, and they had danced a few times, so he thought for sure they would be going out sometime soon. This was just another example of Gianni having bad luck with girls, and the bad luck continued for him.

Gianni got his first full-time job, and it was located in downtown Chicago. It was in a high floor in one of those big downtown skyscraper buildings, and the view from the window was amazing to him. His first job out of the grocery store and into an office setting. This job would teach him all the basics he needed to continue in the same field of finance throughout his career. He began to get friendly with different people in different departments in the office, and he was liking the fact that he was not just regulated to sitting behind his computer and was able to communicate with others. During his last year he spent working at his first full-time job, one girl who recently started working there as an executive administrator—her name was Cassandra—began to get friendly with Gianni. Gianni thought she was a very nice woman. She was always smiling and always said hello when she passed over his desk. And Gianni would be friendly right back with her when he would walk over by her desk. He not only thought she was friendly, but he also thought she had a terrific figure. She was voluptuous, and her face was pretty in his opinion, and for Gianni he had decided long before she started working with him that he would never pursue a woman he worked with after what had happened with Denise when he worked at the grocery store. Although he was friendly with Cassandra, he certainly would not be asking her out on a date anytime soon, but they were friends.

After working several years at his full-time job, Gianni gave his resignation after working at this company for several years to pursue another job offer, and he would be saying goodbye to many of his colleagues at the office. They had a goodbye and good-luck party for him after work. Cassandra felt that they were too good of friends for a group goodbye sendoff and asked him if he would join her after the goodbye party for some appetizers and a drink for a more personal goodbye. Gianni didn't mind this offer since they were friends, and he did not have plans for the evening. They went to this restaurant a few blocks away from where the office had held his goodbye party, and they sat down and began to order drinks and appetizers. They began to talk about his new exciting opportunity and what was going on with her. She told him that, just recently, she moved to an apartment not far from the office and was loving this new lifestyle of living downtown and working downtown. Gianni said that it was awesome that someone was living the lifestyle they had been seeking; he felt the same for himself except that his family and friends and his lifestyle called for him to be working and living in the suburbs.

He was rather surprised to hear that she was not dating anyone at that point, and she said she was surprised that he was not seeing anyone himself. He responded with it was not because he was lacking any effort to date someone but also the issue was that he was still trying to get over his breakup with his girlfriend and had not met anyone he wanted to start that special loving relationship with. And so far, his dates have gone badly for him. She said she understood and sometimes it took a while for someone to get over a heartbreak, and it would take a special person to help get over that pain. And maybe she might have some medication for that pain and just had a big smile on her face after she said that. He felt that she may have just begun to flirt with him. Or was it just his imagination or wishful thinking on his part?

The appetizers and drinks were about to come to an end, and Cassandra then asked Gianni if he would like to check out her new apartment she moved into since the night was still young, and she was enjoying their conversation. Her apartment was located within walking distance to where they were. Gianni agreed that the night was still young, and he was also enjoying the conversation they were having and would not mind seeing her new place. They arrived at her apartment, and she gave him the grand tour of her place. And he thought her apartment was very nice, and he loved the fact that she had a balcony because it reminded him of when he went back to Italy to visit his family, and it seemed every relative of his had a place with a balcony. She then asked if he'd like a glass of wine because she wanted a glass herself, and he accepted her offer. She came back to the balcony, and they drank wine and talked some more. As it was getting later, and the air was getting chilly, she told Gianni that they should go inside on the couch because she was getting cold. So they moved inside on the couch and continued with their drinking and talking. Then Cassandra said if he would excuse her because she needed to change her clothes and get more comfortable after a long day at the office. Gianni was feeling a little buzzed from the drinking at the restaurant, and now they would be adding wine into the mix at her apartment. His imagination started to get a little wild and began to think women have been so aggressive with him that he thought for sure she was going to come out in some sexy lingerie outfit and was getting ready for the two of them to get it on! Well, she came back out of her bedroom, but it was nowhere near what he had pictured—she had a white T-shirt and black sweats. So much for his imagination.

She sat down again, and they continued their conversation. Cassandra reacted to Gianni who seemed distracted and asked him if there was anything wrong? Gianni told her there was absolutely nothing wrong, but he couldn't help but notice that her nipples were rather hard and large and very noticeable poking through her T-shirt. She started laughing, saying, "What's wrong? Haven't you ever seen hard nipples before?"

He said of course he had, but he just never saw nipples of her proportion! She said she was sorry, but the air was chilly and that was what happened when there was chilly air and a handsome Italian man in front of her. She then lifted her top to give Gianni the full view of her nipples and breasts. And then she moved up on his lap, and she said he should help warm up her nipples and pushed her large breasts toward his mouth to warm them up for her! Who was Gianni to deny such a request? And he began to warm up her nipples and the rest of her and himself as well. One thing led to another, and before he knew it he was having sex with Cassandra! It was definitely a hot evening of sex, and they were both enjoying each other physically. She seemed to be feeling very comfortable with sex and with Gianni, and that made him feel at ease and able to enjoy the pleasure of sex with her.

That could be attributed to the fact that they were not strangers, and so between them working together and finding each other attractive and some sexual tension had built up between them. And they were also buzzed from their drinking probably, which made for a comfortable evening of sex for them. For the first time in a long time, Gianni was able to have sex with a woman and not feel guilty about it after the fact since his breakup with Stephanie. And now, maybe now, he could build on this momentum with the next woman. And maybe Cassandra was the medicine that he needed to get over the pain of his breakup with Stephanie. And although he never saw Cassandra again, he was feeling pretty good and confident about his future and finding a woman to start a relationship with.

Gianni started working full-time in the suburbs of Chicago and worked for a big corporation. He was excited because of the location and the company he was working for. Great opportunity, great work culture, and great benefits also. What he was not expecting was the attention he would soon be getting at the office. After a couple months, the office had just opened their operations at the current location he was working at, and Gianni began to make friends with some of his coworkers. Gianni in general was a friendly guy and made friends rather easily. One of the departments at the office seemed to have the most attractive group of women working together, and two of the women would end up paying Gianni a lot of attention.

Gianni went on his break with a group of coworkers he became friends with, and when the break was over, he and his buddy Caleb headed back to their desks, as they were entering the elevator to return to their desks, who should happen to take the same elevator as them but Delilah? She was one of the girls from the department that had the most attractive women. She was also returning to her desk from her break. Caleb and Gianni looked at each other, smiling at the fact that she was in the elevator with them. All of a sudden, the elevator got stuck on the way up to their floor, and that was the first time she had spoken to Gianni and Caleb. They began making comments such as they were hoping not to get stuck in there for a very long, and finally after a few minutes of being stuck the elevator started up again, and they were off to their floor and desks. When Gianni and Caleb were about to make their way back to their desks, Caleb said, "Hey, Gianni, I would not have minded at all if we were stuck in the elevator a little longer with her."

And Gianni said, "Oh yeah, I would not mind that at all as well!"

Delilah and Gianni had their first conversation in the elevator, although a rather short chat. And the other girl who paid a lot of attention to Gianni was named Carolina, and both women were very attractive, but Carolina had already spoken with Gianni on a few occasions. Since he had this elevator ride with her and they had spoken, it was as if this was not just by chance that they got stuck in the elevator together. Rather, it was destiny for them to start speaking with each other, and before he realized it he was walking past her desk, and she and him would exchange hello. And then the hellos would soon turn into small conversations, and they began to learn about each other. It turned out that Delilah had studied in Italy and knew how to speak Italian. And so she was able to converse with Gianni in English and Italian. And well, Gianni was enjoying speaking with her.

He would find excuses to have to walk past Delilah's desk on a daily basis, and he would make sure he had to walk past her desk, so he could see her and say hello. And almost every time he stopped to chitchat with her, and it was a nice little chat, and they would smile and laugh as they would be asking how their day was going. One afternoon when Gianni took a stroll over to her desk, this time when he stopped over at her desk it would not be a typical visit. There was a divider wall tall enough where he could put his arm at the top and even lay his chin on his arms. And as she was sitting speaking with him, when she suddenly squeezed her breasts together to give Gianni a more insightful view of breasts and cleavage, now Gianni's eyes nearly popped out of his head from the surprise view. And now he knew this woman had the hots for him, and that this was not just two people speaking friendly to each other.

Gianni walked back to his desk and began to think about what he should do now. Clearly she liked him, but he had a rule about not going out with girls he worked with. But then he thought to himself, *What is the big deal? A cup of coffee or a drink. No biggie, right?* And so he looked up her extension for her phone, and he dialed it. And when she picked up, he proceeded to ask her if she would like to get coffee or drinks after work sometime soon. And she said, "Well, how about tomorrow after work?"

He said he was free and was looking forward to getting together with her, and they decided to grab dinner and drinks at an establishment near the office. It was on a Friday evening, and he thought it was a perfect start to the weekend. They spoke about their background and how much she loved her studies in Italy, the Italian people, the culture, the food, and of course the handsome men like Gianni! She got rather flirtatious with Gianni by saying things he certainly was not expecting to hear, and she noticed he seemed a little taken back by some of the things she was saying. Gianni proceeded to tell her that he just was not used to someone speaking so freely, at least not in a setting like they were in—dinner, drinks, a date—and he was just adjusting to it.

She said, "Well, don't you feel it is important to be honest and speak freely?"

Gianni said sure, but not all women liked a man to speak so freely, and many were overly sensitive especially when it came to explicit things. Delilah said, "Hmm, why don't we give it a test?"

Gianni said, "What do you mean give it a test? Like how?"

She said, "Well, why don't you think about the most explicit thing you have had or been having about me and say it to me? No-holds-barred, say exactly how you thought it."

Gianni thought to himself that he really was not having any explicit thoughts to that point, but he turned to see if anyone was nearby and then proceeded to say, "I was thinking I bet your pussy tastes really sweet."

And she had a big smile and said to Gianni, "I see you are blushing from saying it!"

He said, yeah, the women he has had relationships with or been on dates in his life had been rather subtle when it came to saying explicit things or simply didn't like a guy to say such things to them.

Delilah said, well, she grew up in a different culture, and sex and sexuality was not looked down on in that society. Delilah then said to Gianni, "Well, I must respond to what you were thinking and tell you that, yes, you are correct. My pussy does taste really sweet. And I would like you to taste it for yourself. But only if I get to taste your Italian cock and then feel it in my sweet pussy!"

Gianni almost fell back over his chair when she said that, and it was the most explicit thing he ever had a woman say to him. Dana was the closest woman that said explicit things to him, but they were never on a date. And then Delilah said to him, "So how about it? Why don't we go back to my place, and we can explore each other and fulfill our passionate lust for each other?"

Gianni responded with "But of course" and then screamed out, "CHECK PLEASE!"

They went back to her place, and it was not a disappointment to Gianni. After all, he had been attracted to Delilah since she began working at the office. And all that flirting that had been going back and forth at the office and now from the restaurant definitely was a gateway to a night of passionate sex. After they entered her apartment, they began to kiss, hot and heavy, and before he knew it she was ripping his and her clothes off, and she pushed him down onto the couch and jumped on top on him to continue their hot kissing. And then she grabbed him by the hand to guide him over to her bedroom, and there was no doubt she was aggressive and leading how things were progressing between the two. They continued kissing passionately as they stood by her bed, and then she pushed him down and said to him, "Lie down." And so he obliged her command, and she then proceeded to move toward and said, "You wanted to taste my pussy. Well, here you go." And she sat on his face. She said, "I told you my pussy was sweet." And then she said, "Now it's time I get a taste of your Italian cock." She maneuvered her body into the sixty-nine position, and they continued on with their oral sex.

The sex that followed the oral session was hot, and it seemed to go on all night long. She was even more lustful than he was imagining and was even more expressive during their sexual session. The next morning, as Gianni was getting ready to head home after a most terrific evening with Delilah, she was passionate, flirtatious, lustful, and definitely enjoyed saying explicit things. She began to mention to him if he knew she was in the United States on a work visa, and he said yeah, he had heard that before. She then told him it would expire the next week and it did not look like it would be renewed by the company and that would have to go back home to her country.

He was saddened when he heard that news from Delilah. Just when he finally made a move and the move paid off for him, it was suddenly over for him. It was a good thing Gianni had not gotten himself too emotionally attached to her and then been heartbroken from this scenario. He initially did not think if it would be a long-term opportunity, since he had heard about her being in the country on a work visa, but one never knows how quickly things can change. He has had two straight sexual experiences that did not turn into anything more than just a sexual experience, but he was not feeling any guilt trip about doing so. And now he knew that he was over Stephanie, and then he chalked this experience with Delilah as yet another woman that would not work out in the long run for him.

So with Delilah being gone, this seemed to give an opening to Carolina to be even more aggressive toward Gianni at the office. She began telling others at the office how she liked him and Gianni liked her and that she was just waiting for Gianni to ask her out. Kind of like planting the idea in his head by rumors! About a little over a year after Gianni had starting working at this office, the company would soon be closing down, and layoffs were imminent for him, and most of the staff would also get their walking papers. So he was pretty upset since he really liked working at this office and for the company. The last few weeks was very rough on most that were working at the office, and so on the very last day there were discussions about going to the unemployment office as a group. And Carolina walked over to Giannis's desk and said she would join their group to head over to the unemployment office. Sure enough, they all drove over to the unemployment office to apply for the unemployment benefits. And then Carolina said to Gianni, "We need to keep in touch, maybe hang out together. Here is my number. What is your number?" So they exchanged numbers, and before Gianni knew it, he was heading out for drinks and movies with Carolina. It was like, damn, he didn't even put in the effort. She sort of guided him to make suggestions, and all of a sudden he found himself hanging out with her and not just as friends—at least not in her eyes. One day Carolina gave Gianni a call and asked him when they would get together again. He began to mention to her that since he had so much free time on his hands that he decided to visit his family in Italy in a couple weeks because he received a severance package from work and hadn't had a vacation in a long time. And so they decided to meet up on the upcoming Saturday before he left for his trip to Italy.

They decided that, since it was October and Halloween was the holiday coming up in a couple weeks and he wouldn't be around because he would be in Italy, they decided to check out a haunted house and then head out for drinks at a local bar. They went to the bar after the haunted house and spoke some more and drank some, and they were feeling a good buzz going from the alcohol. She asked if they could go back to her place to end their evening by watching a movie on her couch. They went back to her place, and they sat on the couch, turned on the TV, and then she told him she needed to change into something more comfortable. He had heard that line before, and she came back with tight-fitting workout sweats, and she sat rather close to him. And before he knew it, she grabbed his hand, and she placed it directly on her butt and gestured him to rub his hand back and forth. And then after a while of rubbing her butt cheeks, he decided to see where else she would like his hand to be rubbing, and he moved toward her breasts and began to squeeze one at a time. He could hear her moan in pleasure, and she moved up to kiss, and they began kissing and touching. Before he knew it, she was unzipping his pants to give him a blow job. And after performing oral sex on Gianni, she grabbed him by the hand and guided him to her bedroom. As they entered her bedroom, she then told to him fuck her brains out like there was tomorrow! Gianni was surprised because this was seemingly going so fast, and he never even intended to see or date Carolina in the first place. But he swore to himself that he would just go with the flow, and he did. They had sex, and it was hot. She was not shy about her sexual hunger in the bedroom and wanted Gianni to be as hot and wild as he wanted to be with her because she was hot for him!

A few days after his date with Carolina and just a few days before he would be heading out to Italy for his long-awaited vacation, she called up Gianni and then proceeded to tell him she needed a favor from him. He then asked what was the favor that she needed from him. In his mind he was thinking that she needed some help with moving something heavy or going over and giving her a personal goodbye before he left for Italy, and then she proceeded to tell him that he of course was aware that she was in the process of starting a business back in the country where she was originally from, in the Dominican. And as he might recall her telling him, her identity was stolen recently, and she could not secure a loan from the bank. She was hoping he would be willing to lend her the money. Gianni was surprised about this request, and this was the first he was hearing about this new business and her moving back home. He told her he couldn't possibly do that right now since he was not working and was about to head out of the country himself for a month, and that he might have a different answer when he returned. She then said she needed to secure a loan immediately for her opportunity, and he then said, "If you need my answer now, then the answer must be no." He said he would get back in touch with her when he returned, but as he thought about more analytically, the whole loan and business and the Dominican, he began to think why would anyone give a loan to someone who was about to start a business in a foreign country? Will he ever see her again and get repaid? Was the last date he had with her where they had sex a way of her to make him feel close and obligated to lend her money?

Gianni went to Italy and began to gather his thoughts and his experience with love and a relationship while he was vacationing, and he started thinking about his past relationships and the fact that now there were three women in a row that he worked with and became friends with that have gone on to something physical, and then that was as far as it would go for him. He took a walk alone on his grandfather's farm in Campagna. It was early evening, and he walked over to his favorite piazza, and he sat at the fountain to think deeply and assess so far his love life and what he or where he has erred with the women.

He seemed to break out of his shyness and now had successfully asked girls out on a date. He no longer felt guilty about being with a woman other than Stephanie, so he seemed to be on the right path to recovery. Then he began to think about a song that tore him up emotionally, and the song was "Girl I Am Searching for You" by Stevie B. And certainly most of the words resonated with how he was feeling, how he was searching for a girl, and how the girls he met were over for him before they ever really got started. And now this seemed to have been going on well over five years since his breakup with Stephanie. Gianni felt like he would never find his true love or that she would never show her face to him and that it was all a fantasy. His cousins could that tell something was bothering Gianni, and he told them about his bad luck with relationships and girls recently, and the last girl he had seen she used him and tried to get money from him and how offended he was that she thought he was so gullible that he would give her the money, but clearly it was money that was her motive for her aggressiveness of Gianni. He was also hoping this was not starting to become a trend with women he'd meet in the future because then his optimism to meet a woman and fall in love would be very slim. His monthlong vacation in Italy flew by quickly, and then it was over, and it was time to return to Chicago. It was time to find a new job and get back into the normal life of working daily, and he decided he would not be contacting Carolina and that he would not be giving her any money even though he came to that decision a couple days before he got to Italy and was no longer going to bother with Carolina again because he felt she used sex as a way to try and persuade him to give her money when she asked for it.

Gianni returned to working for a company in downtown Chicago and began to get friendly with several people at this office. The company's main corporate office was located where he was working, and the company had a second office a few floors down from where this office was located. They needed all this office space because the company was a sales-based company. Too many sales reps to fit into one office, so they had two offices: one for the administration where Gianni worked, and the second office was for the sales reps. And they also had reps in two other cities outside of Illinois, a total of four offices. A short time after starting at the company, there was a small party after work for both offices in Chicago for employees to get together and to mingle and create a cohesiveness for everyone. He had become friendly with the executive assistant, and her name was Jordyn. And there was also a receptionist at the second office, and so she saw him and began to approach Gianni and said, "Excuse me, but we have not been introduced. I am Jasmine."

And Gianni introduced himself, and he thought she was just absolutely gorgeous, like a step above him. He felt like she was out of his league! He and Jordyn started hanging out together outside the office as they would go out to lunch together, and she would tell him some very personal things and how she was struggling with her boyfriend, so they began getting close.

One day she went up to Gianni and said she had a story to tell him, but it would have to wait—she would have to tell him later during lunch. They sat down and began to have lunch at a food court, when she began to tell Gianni that she had a dream the previous night and that he was in it! Gianni could not believe his ears. He proceeded to ask her, "What was I doing in your dream?" Jordyn told him that she couldn't find her boyfriend and then she headed over to where Gianni and his friends were playing cards. "And since you are Italian, you might know some people who might be able to able to tell me the status of my boyfriend." In the dream she continued on to say that he went into the backroom of the Italian coffee shop where he and his friends were hanging out, and he spoke with someone who might be able to provide some insight, and he came back to her where she was sitting and waiting at in the coffee shop and he said to her he was not sure how to tell her but from what he just heard from the folks in the backroom, her boyfriend is a bad boy and, well, she should probably proceed to find a new guy to be her boyfriend. And she said she feared it would be that kind of bad news, and since she was single now, would he be interested in being her new boyfriend? Well, he said yes, he was interested in being her boyfriend and would not disappoint her by disappearing on her. That was the dream Jordyn had and then looked at Gianni for a reaction, and he just sat there mouth open and not knowing what to say. Then she said, "So what do you think about that crazy dream I had?"

He said, "Yeah, that was a crazy dream. It sounded like a scene from one of those mob movies or mob shows. You got over your boyfriend real fast and found another man quickly." And they laughed.

Although Gianni and Jordyn had a big laugh about the dream she had about him, he couldn't help but wonder if that was some kind of subconscious thought, or if this dream actually happened as she described and that she was hoping to be hinting to him that he should make a move on her, so she could dump her boyfriend. A few months later, the company was having their annual convention, and it was being held out of state. Jordyn oversaw the booking of the hotel and rooms for everyone to stay for this weeklong convention. There was one catch: because the company had four different offices, the owner wanted people to share rooms to cut the costs of the convention for the company. Jordyn then asked Gianni if he would room with her, since they were good friends, and she really didn't have any other friends or would be comfortable sharing a room with someone else. Gianni couldn't believe it. Wow, someone he was not in a relationship with was asking him to share a room with him. And since they were friends, he agreed to this arrangement! Gianni had no idea what or how this convention would go, since he had never been to one in the past, so he was not sure what to expect from the weeklong convention but that he at least would be meeting some other employees from the other two offices that he had spoken with on the phone.

The weeklong convention finally arrived, and it was not what Gianni had pictured it might have been. During the day it was meetings all day long, speeches, or more like inspirational speeches to motivate the salespeople to sell more! Well, this was certainly not in Giannis's interest since he was not a salesperson, so these speeches were rather uninspiring to him and rather boring to him. And Jordyn very much agreed, since she also was not a salesperson and part of her reasoning. She said she didn't want to room with a salesperson. The last night of the convention, Jordyn and Gianni began drinking a little more than they had been drinking the nights before, and so by the time they were done drinking, they both were pretty buzzed and could barely walk back to their room. Lucky for them, they did sober up enough, so they could find their way back to their room. And once they got into the room, they both tripped and fell to the floor together. And before Gianni knew it, they were kissing each other on the floor. And then it turned hot and heavy, and a night of sex followed. He certainly was not even thinking about anything other than he was buzzed, and he was turned on, and this was certainly not planned or what he had in mind. The next day, they both woke up with hangovers and packed up to go home. And while at the airport waiting to board, both finally spoke about last night, and both said it was a drunken mistake and to never speak about this again. Gianni promised he would never speak of it again or tell any of his friends about this. As much as he would have liked to continue to see Jordyn as her boyfriend, he knew that it was not going to happen, and he was hoping this incident would not interfere in their relationship they had at work.

One of Gianni's newest friends he was hanging out with was Jake, who worked at the first company he worked full-time with, and they continued to stay friends and hang out together. Since Jake was still working downtown and so was Gianni at this point, they both took the same train line home, and they decided to ride the train together one night after work. Jake was beginning to tell him about the problems he was having with his girlfriend and was hoping he could get some advice from Gianni. For Gianni, this was certainly still new territory, and the last time he gave advice on girls his friend Johnny from high school blew up in his face. But since Jake was a little younger and Gianni was a little older and more experienced than him, he figured he might be able to help him out.

As they were sitting in the train and coming to a conclusion to Jake's problems, the train made a stop at one of the scheduled stops. All of a sudden two girls entered the train. They sat down a few seats away from them, and Gianni and Jake look at each other as if to both say, "Nice-looking girls there." The train begins moving, and within a few seconds later the girls got up and moved toward the two empty seats right directly in front of Gianni and Jake. The seats were designed where passengers would be looking at the back of the heads of the passengers in front of them, but these girls turned around to face Gianni and Jake.

Gianni started laughing hysterically. He put his hand on his head and laughed, as Jake's jaw had fallen practically down on the floor, and one of the girls started saying, "Hello? What is so funny?"

Jake said, "Yeah, Gianni, what is so funny?"

And Gianni said, "Oh nothing." He was just thinking of something funny when they happened to sit next to them, but in reality he was just laughing because this was another case of him minding his own business, and women would just come up to him. Gianni did not bother asking for their phone numbers; he just chalked it up as another crazy occurrence that happened in his daily life. Once again, though, one of his friends got to see girls get aggressive with Gianni, and the legend continued to grow!

One of Gianni's friends he made back in his days at the grocery store was his friend Dino, and they hung out a lot, and some of his friends formed a softball team. Gianni was captain of this softball team, so all the guys on the team got pretty close. The guys got close as each year passed during their softball days, and they would hang out with family and friends and girlfriends and so on. One day, Gianni and Jake were out at the mall and shopping for some computer parts when out of the corner of his eye he noticed a girl at the end of the aisle and thought she looked familiar to him. His eyes were not playing tricks with his mind, and she saw him and approached him and began to say, "Hi, you do recognize me, right?"

Gianni responded with "Yeah, I do recognize you. I am just having a difficult time remembering your name and how I know you."

She then said, "Lucy. You know, your friend Dino's girlfriend. I mean his ex-girlfriend."

Gianni then said, "Oh yeah, Dino. Oh hey, how are you doing? I was not expecting to see you here." Gianni said he was sorry to hear about what happened with her and Dino, and she then responded by saying she was not sorry, and it was for the better. And then she said, "So hey, what are you up to these days? Are you seeing anyone?"

Gianni responded by telling her that he was not seeing anyone at that time, and she then said, "Well, here is my number. Give me a call sometime, and we can get together sometime and talk some more. But I have to get going now. It was nice seeing you, and talk with you soon."

She walked away and Jake said, "Oh dude, you are so smooth. You pick girls up so easy. How do you do that?" Jake kept going on. "Dude, first the girls on the train, and now this here at the mall. Wow, you make no effort!" Jake then asked Gianni, "Are you going to call her?"

Gianni told him that there was no way in hell he was going to call her because she was Dino's ex, and he does not go into that territory. He would never date the woman that one of his friends had been in a relationship with, and this was a steadfast rule he lived by to avoid any kind of drama. He told Jake he had enough drama as it is in life and did not need to add on to it. It was kind of funny to Gianni how Jake was admiring him because he thought he was a smooth operator, but he did not do anything to warrant this smooth operator reputation because what Jake witnessed was the girls being the operators.

Gianni found a new job and would be working in the suburbs soon again, and he tendered his resignation to the current company he was working at. And while he was working there, when he was not busy hanging out with Jordyn, he noticed a very attractive redhead in the building he worked in. The office was in a skyscraper, so there were thousands of people that would go in and out of the building on a daily basis. This redheaded woman he noticed several times over the year while he was working for this sales company, he saw her in the building lobby. He saw her at restaurants where he would go grab a bite to eat, so it seemed he had seen her often but always from afar. By the end of the first week of his handing in his resignation, he was riding on the train heading home, and as usual the train was heavily packed. And it wasn't until about five stops or so until his stop that he noticed the mysterious redhead from his building just happened to be sitting a few seats away, and then he started contemplating his plan of action, if he should approach her and strike up a conversation with her.

All he knew was that he was getting nervous. He usually didn't approach women, especially women he'd never spoken with before, and he began to wonder what stop she would be getting off and how much time he had to make his move. He began to wonder if she would be getting off at his stop and if she was living in his neighborhood or close by. And while he was figuring all that out, what do to, the train reached the last stop before Gianni's stop. And she was still on! He saw her get up heading toward the exit for the next stop his stop, and now he figured that this was a sign and that he had to make his move now! He got up to walk over to her, and now he had the right moment to strike up a conversation with her. As he was about to say something, she started to speak to Gianni and said, "Excuse me, but don't you work at the Clark Building?"

Gianni could barely keep a straight face after she said the exact same thing as he was about to say to her, and once again he did not have to make the first move with a woman and then he said to her, "That is so funny, I was just about to ask you the same thing!" He told her, "Yes, I do."

And then she told him, "Yeah, that's what I thought. I saw you a few times in the building and in other places."

And he thought to himself, *This beautiful woman noticed me from afar just as I noticed her.* He was in awe and started thinking, what a small world we live in.

She then asked, "What floor do you work on?"

He said, "Oh I work on the thirty-fifth floor."

And then she asked, "Oh what department are you in?"

And he told her he was in the finance department.

And she responded with "I didn't know finance was on the thirty-fifth floor."

And then Gianni realized that she thought they worked for the same company. And then he told her, "Oh no, wait a minute. You must think we work for the same company. But I don't believe we work for the same company."

She said, "Oh, okay." And then he began to tell her what company he worked for and then proceeded to ask her where she grew up. Turned out she also lived in the same area as him, and he then proceeded to introduce himself.

"By the way, my name is Gianni." She said her name was Erin, and they both said it was a pleasure to finally speak to one another. He said he hoped she would have a great weekend, and he would see her next week, and she said thanks and looked forward to it. Gianni got into his car and then realized he made a big mistake by not coming right out then and there by asking her for her phone number, and now he had one week to run into her again at the office building or on the train or during lunch, and he then he realized that the odds might not be in his favor of that happening. The final week passed, and unfortunately for him he did not run into her again that whole last week he was there.

He was so impressed by the fact that this beautiful woman noticed him as he had noticed her and that he lost his logical way of thinking while they were talking on the train. And he also had gotten so used to women setting the tone that these little and important details like asking for a phone number slipped through his fingers. He liked this girl, and now she was gone forever. He couldn't help but think about the song "Send Me An Angel" by B-Cap. He just thought to himself that he was looking for his angel to be sent, and maybe she might be the angel he was looking for. But he made a mistake and thought that it was not just a chance meeting, since he had seen her so many times. And surely he would see her once more before his last day. But sadly it turned into another missed opportunity for him when all was said and done for him.

CHAPTER 5

The internet and computer age were hitting their peak because of how the internet and cell phones were changing how people were communicating with each other, and Gianni was no exception to this trend. In the late 1990s, Gianni had been chatting with women from chat rooms, and the instant messenger allowed him to develop these virtual friendships. And one such friendship that came from his AOL days of chatting and instant messages was with a girl name Kelly in the early summer of the early 2000s. The uniqueness of Kelly was she lived in California and was about five years older than Gianni. They chatted daily it seemed, and they would discuss personal things about what was happening in their lives, such as work or girlfriend/boyfriend, or friends and family. He found it comforting to just be able to talk to someone about his struggles with love and relationships that he felt he could not speak with anyone close to him at that point.

The newest twist of the internet and computer age in the 2000s was that now there were dating sites. It was as if the personal ads from the newspaper days had moved from newspapers to the internet but with a few modifications, and internet dating sites provided the opportunity for people to communicate with one another at a much faster pace, and their profiles would also allow them to post their photos. Those were the biggest advantages from the newspaper personals. At one point he found a website for singles, but the website he found was specifically catering for those that were Italian and looking to date Italians, and this site he found had a lot of subscribers that were looking for other Italians to date. He came across one profile and before he knew it, they were exchanging e-mails and cell phone numbers, and then they agreed to finally meet in person. Her name was Jessica. He told Kelly about this dating website he had found and began to tell her about how he was communicating with Jessica, and they were about to meet. Gianni met Jessica, and their first meeting and their date got off to a great start. They got along really well, they had a great conversation, and they had plenty of laughter. And they were attracted to one another, and they would be looking forward to their next date.

After a couple dates, Jessica told Gianni that she would be spending time with her family over at her mother's house, and if he would like to come over and meet her family and then afterward the two of them could go out and spend the evening together. This caught Gianni by surprise, especially meeting family after just two dates. And so he began to think, wow, she did like him and was making the rounds of getting into a serious or committed relationship. Gianni was starting to feel comfortable with how things were progressing together. In fact, it seemed to be going faster than he was anticipating it would. He arrived where Jessica was waiting for him at her mom's house, and then he got introduced to her family. And after a little while of conversation, Jessica told everyone that she and Gianni were heading out for the evening.

They headed out to his car, and they drove out toward her place for their date to begin, to begin their evening. He parked his car near her place, and they walked over to the restaurant nearby and sat down to have dinner and have their conversation. She began flirting a little with Gianni, which she had not done prior, and now she began saying little things to him like how the thought of them kissing after dinner was turning her on and that her nipples were getting very hard that they might poke through her top! Gianni was surprised by her saying these things since she had not spoken with him in that flirtatious manner. He was really starting to get comfortable, feeling like she was into him, and he was beginning to let his guard down some since he met her family. She was being flirtatious and that she must be very comfortable with him as well!

They finished up their dinner, and they headed back to her place for some after-dinner wine. They sat down and drank some wine, and Gianni decided to continue with the flirting by saying he could tell she was turned on because he could see her very hard nipples trying to poke through her top! She then proceeded to say to him that, oh yes, she was very turned on but not because of the thought of them kissing, but she had been turned on since she noticed his package in his pants and was very impressed with his package! Gianni started smiling and laughing and was trying to figure out what he should say next and return the flirtatious talk. And then he asked her when did she notice his package? She told him that while they were driving, she snuck a peak toward his crotch and noticed it and began to get excited and turned on! Gianni then responded to her by saying, "Well, I am glad you are impressed, and maybe you can unwrap my package and get yourself a closer look at it!"

She laughed and said, "That is the best idea I have heard all day." And she moved over toward him and began to kiss and feel Gianni, and her hands headed down toward his pants to unzip his pants, so she could get a closer view of his package. And she then said, "Wow, even more impressive than I initially was thinking!"

Gianni then asked, "Oh, do you like?"

She then said, "*Me like*" and began to give him a blow job. After a while of giving Gianni oral sex, Jessica then said, "Why don't we go to my bedroom, so we can explore more?"

And he responded with "Okay, sounds good."

And she then said, "Wait, I will need to grab a couple towels. It will probably get very wet." And she was very hot! Gianni could not believe his ears. Wow, he was thinking, and he certainly did not have any idea that they were going to have sex that night. He was looking forward to more nights like this one!

Gianni told Kelly about how things were going with Jessica and how excited he was about meeting her and how well things were progressing. He met her mother and her brothers and nephews and nieces, and finally he felt like he met someone he would be settling down with. A week had passed since Gianni had met Jessica's family, and the last time he had seen her as well, when he got a call from Jessica and then after a couple minutes, she asked Gianni how he thought things were going between the two of them. He told her that he thought things were going really well, and she then told him that she did not agree with his assessment. and then she told Gianni that she had to break things off with him. And then, adding insult to injury, not only did she break things off with him, but she also then proceeded to insult him, which caught him off guard. In life, no matter how many girls he had failed with in a relationship or broken off with, the one thing about his breakups were that they were rather amicable—usually a woman would say something to the affect that he was a really nice guy or a sweet guy.

Jessica, however, took a different route in the breakup call. She told him that when they were together, she found him rather boring, and the dates were very bland—nothing exciting, just sitting and talking for the most part. And she needed someone exciting to keep her interest, plus they grew up with different backgrounds. So she told him that he was boring, and the conversations they had were superficial at best, but none of those things she was saying made any sense to Gianni because they grew up in the same neighborhood, they had similar Italian American backgrounds, neither grew up rich or poor, and as far as the lack of excitement and superficial conversations she complained about—why did she bother to continue to go out with him after the first date? Or why was she so turned on by him the last time they were together, and turned on so much so that they had engaged in sex? And of course none of this was making any sense to him. He was terribly upset about this whole thing with Jessica and needed to talk to someone, and that someone was Kelly.

He began telling Kelly how upset Jessica made him, and then she said, "Hey, let's talk on the phone and discuss it there rather than type this out."

And he said that was a great idea. They began to talk, and Gianni just completely lost it and began bawling on the phone. He could not believe what Jessica had told him and did not understand why she would say the things she said; he had never been hurt like that. He had been hurt before emotionally from his breakup with Stephanie, but this one really stung him—the insults, he never experienced insults before. From what Kelly could tell, she had a feeling that since the breakup happened so soon after he met her family that they did not approve of him, or they were not impressed by him. And that probably meant more to her than anything else. "Why else would she suddenly break it off and then start launching a myriad of insults to hurt you and to distract you from the fact that things were going so good with the two of you." Kelly continued on to tell him if she just said she needed to move on to date other men, then she would sound like a slut or whore. "But if she insults you instead, she will feel better about herself and avoid feeling guilty about dumping a nice guy."

Gianni thanked Kelly for listening to him, and when he got off the phone, he began to think about what Kelly was saying and thought she was making a lot of sense and perhaps she was onto something about Jessica. After that initial phone call, Kelly and Gianni spoke on the phone on a regular basis and spent less time too on the instant messaging, and they became friends over the years. One song that helped Gianni recover from the heartbreak of Jessica was the Lou Rawls song "You'll Never Find Another Love Like Mine." He felt that once he was in a committed relationship, he would be true blue and give the attention and respect like no other man would.

Gianni had lost a lot of faith that he was going to meet the woman he would settle down with in his life, especially after the Jessica debacle, and he tried to get over it by keeping himself busy by playing golf or playing cards with his friends or going to Las Vegas with them. On one particular trip out to Las Vegas with his friends, they were celebrating a bachelor party, and this would not be a quiet trip for him, although it seemed it was never quiet for him whether he was home—or anywhere he went, for that matter! On one of those evenings, the guys had dinner plans at a popular steak house as part of their celebratory event for the bachelor, and Gianni got himself showered and readied for the evening. When he headed toward the elevators and went in and as the doors began to close, he saw three women heading for the elevator, and he kept the doors from closing so they also could get in. There he was in the elevator with these three women, and he was minding his own business, and as he got a look at the women he noticed they were older than Gianni and the popular term for women of that age group at that time was "cougar"!

So there he was in an elevator with three attractive cougars, and before he knew it they began to talk to him, and one of them said, "Wow, you are dressed very sharp. What's going on?"

And Gianni responded. And being his polite self that he usually was, he told them about the dinner plans he had, and they responded with "Well, maybe we should join you!"

Gianni giggled, and then one of them said, "Mmmmm…what is that cologne you are wearing? It smells good." Gianni told them he was wearing Armani Code, and one of the women said to him, "Well, that smells really good. And we may not be able to keep our hands off you much longer!"

Gianni could not believe it. For the first time, he had not one but three women at the same time hitting on him! Sure enough, the elevator finally reached the main floor, and they said they would be on the lookout for him since they were all on the same floor and hope they run into each other again!

Gianni was walking over to the restaurant and began to reminisce about the time he was meeting his buddies after being with Stephanie and how that one girl saw him and she invited him up to her hotel room. Although this was not exactly the same scenario, just the fact that he was heading over to meet his buddies and something very shocking happened to him while he was alone, his buddies would probably see the expression on his face when he arrived at the restaurant. He arrived to meet up with the guys at the steak house, and sure enough his friends could tell he wasn't his usual self and asked what was going on, or if there was something wrong.

Gianni said, "Well, you will not believe what happened to me on the way here."

And then Lenny said, "Oh no. Okay, go ahead and tell us what happened."

He proceeded to tell them that he was nearly molested in the elevator by three cougars! He told them about the exchange that just happened in the elevator ride, and their eyes nearly popped out of her heads, and they began to laugh. Lenny said, "Oh this shit only happens to you, Gianni! How many times can these things continue to happen to you?" Lenny proceeded to say, "You know, if the other guys had not told me the other stories prior to this one you just told us, I would have thought you made it up. But being that you are an honest guy and don't bullshit people and the other guys have actually seen these encounters happen, there is no doubt that this elevator encounter actually did happen! Lenny then proceeded to ask Gianni, "Well, you going to see them later?"

Gianni responded and said he did not make plans with the women and that when the elevator doors opened, they went their separate ways. "And I came straight here to meet up with you guys!"

Don, one of the other guys, had to give Gianni a hard time. And of course, he could not resist but tease Gianni a bit and told him, "You mean you chose us guys over women? What is wrong with you? You should had turned around and gone back to your room and been fucking the shit out of them or have at least made plans to meet one of them after our dinner!"

All the guys at the table started laughing and continued teasing Gianni that he did not need to go to a strip club with them and that he had his own harem of women for entertainment! Dinner was over, and Gianni headed back to his hotel, but before going back to his room he decided to try his luck on the slot machines. After a few minutes of playing the slots, who should happen to also come by? None other than the three cougars from the elevator!

Gianni knew this was trouble, and the ladies were buzzing for sure. They all sat near him and began to talk with him and asked him how his dinner was. And he was being polite and told them how his dinner was with his friends, and then he asked them how their evening was, and they said it was almost a perfect night for them, but there was still a chance to end the night perfectly! One of the ladies began to ask if he would be interested in having a little fun with her, and Gianni was thinking to himself, *Well, this woman is attractive.* And he was a little buzzed himself and was in Vegas, so he said, sure why not. He then said, "Why don't you come over to my room in a little while? Let me get a chance to get freshened up first." He also asked them to give him a half hour or so. "My room number is 3469."

He really did not think she would take him up on his offer, but what she said next caught him off guard—she said, "We will be there!"

As Gianni was heading back to his room to wash up, he began to think to himself, *Wait a second, is she really going to show? And wait a minute, did she say, "We will be there"? Or was she kidding? Did she mean we as in two of them, or maybe all three of them?* He said, "Hell, this is Vegas. Seems people go visiting here to go a little crazy while out here!"

Sure enough, Gianni got freshened up and rested on his bed watching TV, figuring the time would come and pass, and no one would be knocking on the door. But then sure enough there was a knock on the door, and he was expecting just the one woman, the one he was speaking to. And to his shock, all three showed up! Then one of them said, "You don't mind that all three of us showed up to have a little fun. Since the three of us find you attractive, it didn't feel it would be fair if only one of us got to have fun with you. We hope you are rested and have taken your vitamins!"

Before he knew it, all three women either had their hands rubbing up on him or began undressing themselves. And before he knew it, they each were finding a way to get their hands, mouths, and their body on him for his pleasure. It was all happening oh so fast that he had no time to even think about what he was doing. And it seemed he was dreaming, but oh it was definitely real! Gianni knew one thing for sure—he could not tell his friends about this. They probably would not believe it. Hell, Gianni could not believe it himself, and he was the one getting the action. But since they were giving him a hard time about walking away from the women, then they might have thought he was only making this story up to make up for them teasing him earlier!

CHAPTER 6

As the internet progressed and more and more dating sites popped up and then eventually turned into phone apps and people meeting from the internet in person became more sociably accepted, there were still the elements that could possibly make for a bad situation. And Gianni over the years had heard about more and more scams and fake profiles that were popping up as more and more people were turning to the internet to find a companion or love. He tried to be as diligent as possible because he did come across some fake profiles: the person, the pictures of the person he was speaking with turned out to be fake, since he actually saw the same person on a modeling site by pure chance!

He signed up for an Italian dating website, and he began talking to someone who appeared to be from Malaysia. He was not sure if this was a fake profile or a genuine person, and so he proceeded with caution and tried to see what she would say or what he thought might lead to confirm to him that she was a fake, or if in fact she was the real deal. Her name was Nadia, and she was from Malaysia, just a few years younger than Gianni. So he then said what was she doing on an Italian website since she didn't seem to be Italian? Was it because she was looking for an Italian man? She said not only was she looking for an Italian man, but she in fact was also part Italian. Turned out her father was from Italy, and so she was half Italian, and the other half on her mother's side she had a variety of ethnicities: Chinese, East Indian, and a couple of others. So when he finally realized she was legitimate and not a fake profile, they both began chatting on a daily basis on messenger. And although the time difference was significant, his evenings was her morning, so they would continue to chat. They even did video chat online, just to see each other live instead of just typing messages to each other.

He was glad they were becoming good friends. They spoke for well over a year by messenger and video. One day Nadia had some big news for Gianni and said she and her cousins were going on vacation, and the country they would be visiting was the United States. They were going to start in California and work their way east to New York, and Chicago was one of the cities that was on the list of the American cities they would be visiting. Nadia then asked Gianni when she got to Chicago, would he like to meet to her? Gianni could not believe the news she just told him. The odds of them meeting in person would be close to astronomical, he felt. After all, they were across the world from each other, and such a trip for someone in Malaysia would be a fairly expensive trip to take. Gianni said he would absolutely meet her. After all, they were friends, and it would be foolish for them not to meet her in person. He said he would treat her to his favorite restaurant and hoped she would enjoy her visit to Chicago and the US, and they were both looking forward to that day!

The day finally arrived, and Gianni was nervous about meeting someone from so far away, from another part of the world. So technically this was his first international date, so to speak. She was staying at a downtown Chicago hotel, and so that was perfect in Gianni's eyes since his favorite restaurant was located close to downtown Chicago. He went into the hotel lobby, they spoke on the cell phone, and he told her where he would be waiting for her in the lobby and what he was wearing. And he anxiously awaited her to finally appear, and lo and behold there she was—Nadia at last in the flesh! They gave each other a big hug hello and said it was a pleasure to meet in person.

He said, "Let's walk over to my favorite restaurant and drink a little vino and enjoy eating the best Italian food Chicago has to offer."

They sat down, and it was no coincidence that this was his favorite restaurant. He and his friends went there so often, the owners and the employees there knew Gianni, and they gave him the extra warm welcome since Gianni was in there with a date—and a very beautiful date indeed she was. Nadia then asked Gianni how often he came to this restaurant because "Everyone here is coming over here to shake your hand and say hello like you were an important person!"

He laughed and said that on many occasions he and his friends from work would eat at this restaurant for lunch almost weekly, sometimes two or three times a week, and the restaurant was within walking distance of the office. But since he hasn't worked at his job since the end of summer, they hadn't seen him in a long time, and they were happy to see him and were asking him where he had been and how he was doing.

He was in awestruck and could not believe how much more beautiful she was in person and her voice, her English accent, was so sexy in his mind—she had that British English-sounding accent. He asked Nadia if she was nervous about finally meeting, and she said she was scared as hell, but after a few minutes after meeting him he made her feel safe. And now that they were sitting together and from the walk they made from the hotel to the restaurant, she felt a certain comfort being with him. She could not explain it—she said he made her feel safe now that she was with him. She also said he was much better looking in person, and he was even more charming than she remembered him being from their previous video chats.

It was the most perfect date he could remember in a long time. They ended up spending the whole evening together, eventually ending up in her hotel room. They were both comfortable with each other together; they felt a special connection together, and not long after they entered the hotel room they sat on the couch at first and began kissing slowly. But then it would turn very passionate, and a few minutes later after their kissing started they moved onto the bed and began to undress each other, continuing with their passionate kissing. As they lay down on the bed and were kissing each other, Nadia then told him that she had been wanting to give him a blow job for a long time and asked him if it was okay if she started with that first.

Gianni said, of course she could start there! The whole evening, it was filled with hot, passionate sex, many different positions, and it was so hot that both of their skin was burning hot and sweating. He opened the window to get some cool air into the room. Good thing it was the fall season for the evening cool air to circulate. Although he spent only two days with Nadia, he would feel that she was his best experience with a woman and sexual experience as well. He had never been turned on as he was when he was Nadia. He was never as hot and sweaty like he was that evening with her, and he just felt the sex experience with her was just at a different level of intensity than his past sexual experiences.

The intensity was probably built up through all the conversations they had online and through their video chats during the year before meeting in person. Perhaps that was what made the transition in person go smoothly between them. He felt so comfortable. In the past the first time he had encountered or went on a date with a woman, there was always an awkwardness at first. But with her, after a couple minutes of the initial face-to-face they were both very comfortable with each other, as if this was not the first time they were together.

The only drawback to this weekend gathering was the fact that they lived halfway around the world from each other, and one of them would have to move to from their home country to live in the other country. And Gianni did not see himself living in Malaysia. And he was not sure if Nadia would want to move to the United States. They spent another day together of the three days she was scheduled to visit Chicago, and it was another great day they spent together and another great evening of hot, passionate sex. She headed back with her cousins to New York to finish their US tour, and both were incredibly sad having to say goodbye to each other. They continued to chat online, and they spoke about how much they both really enjoyed their time together and how much they liked each other. They even spoke about getting together again sometime in the near future, but for Gianni who had just lost his job and was in the middle of trying to find a new job, it was going to be difficult for him to travel.

He told her that once he found a new job, he would see about planning for her to visit Chicago again, except this time he would pay for her trip. As if it were prewritten somewhere, Gianni struggled to find a new job right away, and Nadia began to feel like he was blowing her off, and their chats became less frequent and the amount of time they spent chatting was also less and less during their sessions. And before he knew it, she was dating someone from her country and was getting engaged to be married. Typical outcome for Gianni—when he wanted to be with someone, something goes wrong for him, and it seems that always goes against him. Gianni had one song in mind after all these years of dates with women, different relationships, and after meeting Nadia only one song came to mind for him—"One of These Nights" by the Eagles. Seemed to him the woman he was looking for might have been Nadia, and he let her slip away from his fingers. He felt that they had such great chemistry together, and not since his days with Stephanie did he have this good of a feeling with someone. Unfortunately for him, it was back to the drawing board to searching for that special woman.

As the years passed, after his experience with Nadia, he spent a couple years chatting online with a woman from California, and her name was Milena. She was divorced with kids and was close to his age. She said he was a very good-looking man after seeing his photo and loved the fact that he was Italian American. Gianni saw her photo and thought she was attractive also, and she was having some health issues recently. As Milena and Gianni spent a couple years chatting together online, they would both share their problems and pleasures, and it was a nice friendship they were building together. She managed to get herself back to her normal, healthy ways and began to ask Gianni what was going on in his world these days. He mentioned that he was heading out to Las Vegas with his friends to celebrate his birthday, and she said that it sounded like a lot of fun for his friends to celebrate and hang out. The next day, on their online chat, she said she had an idea and wanted to run it past him but wanted to speak with him on the phone. Gianni agreed to talk with her on the phone, and he then began to suspect that her idea might involve her coming out to Las Vegas to join him on his birthday celebration. She called Gianni and told him she would also like to be in Las Vegas the same weekend that he and his friends would be visiting. And she then also asked him what he thought of her idea and how he would feel about her being there.

Gianni said he had no problem with her being out there at the same time as him, but isn't the real question she should be asking him would it be okay for her to hang out with him? She said yes, that was what she would like to do and join him to celebrate his birthday. And then Gianni said yes, it would be fine, but he warned her that he had plans with his friends. And if she didn't mind hanging out with him when he wasn't with his friends, then that would be a great way to mix up his weekend plans with his friends and now with her, and she agreed with that arrangement. She then proceeded to ask him one more favor. She proceeded to ask him, would he mind if they had sex, no strings attached? She had a new outlook in life after her divorce and near-death experience with her health. And she had this really good feeling about him being not only a wonderful man, but she had this gut feeling he was a great lover. Gianni was taken aback by this request. He was not used to getting such bold requests, but then he proceeded to tell her that he loved sex, and if there is good chemistry and attraction when they meet in Las Vegas in person, then he would definitely have sex with her. Besides, what better gift could one get for their birthday than the pleasure of sex?

The weekend arrived for his Las Vegas trip with his friends to celebrate his birthday, and by the next evening Milena would be arriving, and it was perfect since he and his friends did not have plans set up for Friday night. It was Friday night, and Gianni was feeling the Vegas and his birthday aura and was showered and dressed and ready and just waiting for Milena to come over to his room. She had texted him that she had checked in the hotel and was getting changed and ready for their evening. And finally there was a knock on the door, and there she was in the flesh: looking beautiful, in a sexy outfit, and she looked ready for a night on the town with him. Gianni set the mood for the evening by making reservations at one of his favorite Italian restaurants in Las Vegas.

There was a sexy and romantic setting to the place, the view of the Vegas Strip from the dining table. She told him that the restaurant was just a perfect mood setter for the rest of the evening. Toward the end of the dinner, she proceeded to ask Gianni what he thought of her. Did he find her attractive, and did he feel chemistry? And he said most definitely! He then proceeded to ask how she felt, and she said the feeling was mutual. She was looking forward to going back to his hotel room with champagne chilling and the Jacuzzi and to continue with this wonderful, hot, and seductive setting.

They went back to the hotel room. He grabbed a couple glasses and filled it with the champagne that was on ice chilling, and he then set up the Jacuzzi for them to drink the champagne and soak in the Jacuzzi—a prelude to the hot, passionate sex that would follow next in the Jacuzzi! Then they moved from the Jacuzzi to the bed and continued on with their hot animal sex. She mentioned how she wanted them both to be wild and free with their sex, like animals! Milena was not disappointed with anything: the restaurant, the way he treated her, and making her feel special and her being able to help him celebrate and make his birthday a little more special. And the sex—it could not have been written any better for her and the results that came from this night for her. It was very rare for Gianni to actually have something so planned out as was this trip with Milena, but at the same time he was glad there was not any added pressure for this to be anything more than what they had discussed—nothing long term, just a couple of friends meeting to celebrate his birthday and her recovering back to health and a night of great sex they would not forget!

When in Chicago, Gianni and many of his friends went and loved to go to the same Italian restaurant that he took Nadia to when she was in town, and he and his friends would frequent this restaurant often, and so the staff at the restaurant was not just familiar with Gianni but also his friends. One of Gianni's longtime friends, Lenny, had begun to complain that he kept hearing about this restaurant from him and the other guys, and he demanded to know when they were going to invite him to come along.

Gianni told him, "You pick a day, and we will do lunch there."

And so they picked a day to meet for lunch. Some of the guys were telling Gianni that one of the waitresses at their favorite restaurant was also moonlighting as a waitress at another restaurant, and Gianni knew which waitress they meant since at that time there were only two women that were waitressing at the restaurant. The day arrived for Lenny and Gianni to have lunch at his favorite Italian restaurant, and coincidentally enough the waitress who was doing the moonlighting happened to be their waitress for their lunch. When she walked away while they looked at the menu, Gianni mentioned to Lenny about the moonlighting by the waitress, and he said he was going to say something to her about that just to see what she would say.

She came back to take their orders, and once she took their orders Gianni said to the waitress, "I heard my friends saw you waitressing at another establishment last week."

She smiled and laughed. She knew who his friends were, since they were frequent customers at this place, and she said yes since she worked here during the day. But she needed to make more money, and so she began to pick up extra hours somewhere else in the evenings to make more money and said there was a big difference of environment between the two restaurants.

Gianni wasn't familiar with the environment at the other place, and he told her he had never been at the other place and did not know what she meant. And she said, "Well, you see how this is a family and conservative environment?" She pointed to her blouse being buttoned all the way up to her neck, and she looked around to see if anyone else was around. She then proceeded to unbutton a couple buttons and then grabbed a hold of her breasts inside her shirt and said, "You don't get to see these here!"

And she buttoned up and walked away and put the orders in for them. Gianni and Lenny were certainly not expecting that answer from her and looked at each other and began laughing. Lenny then proceeded to ask if this was something she had done previously, and he said no, that this had never happened before.

Lenny said, "You know, I have known you for many years. And I have heard the stories in the past about how women seem to act differently toward you. And I always get a great laugh, especially when you told us about the three cougars in the elevator in Vegas. And it's not that I didn't believe the stories before, but this is the first time I'd actually seen it for myself. This is the first time I have seen the legend in action with my own eyes, and I could have come in here with anyone else from our group, and she would never had done that. But for some reason you are here, and she does that. And she didn't just show her breasts, she actually showed them directly right at you, completely ignoring me!"

Gianni then said to Lenny, "You know, for years I have witnessed many of these stories you have heard. And if I hadn't been there myself, I also would have a hard time believing them myself. But time after time, something pops up. But it is never the same thing. It is always something different, and it has become almost comical. I mean, look. We are laughing about what just happened. I have been on dates with girls, and waitresses will come up to me, or girls will say something to me when I am with a girlfriend. And I get yelled at by my girlfriend as if it was my fault. Of course, as you witnessed for yourself, women will simply flirt with me. Just like this waitress and other waitresses at other restaurants have done so. And not just waitresses, many other women I have either worked with in the past or gone to school with, time after time these things happen, so nothing really should come as a surprise to me."

Lenny then asked him, "Are you going to ask her for her phone number?"

Gianni said to Lenny that, honestly, he had not even thought about that but probably would not ask for her phone number because he did not have much an interest in her to start with. Lenny threw his arms up and said that if he were single, he would be all over that, and Gianni said, "Well, that's fine. But I am sorry, she does not do it for me!"

After ten years of chatting online and on the phone, Kelly said that since she drove to Las Vegas so often, she would take a ride to meet him the weekend he was visiting for his birthday. Gianni mentioned to her how he was traveling to Las Vegas not to just celebrate his birthday, but that he also needed a few days away from work and from some personal issues he was having with some close friends of his and told her he may not be great company. But she was welcome to join him. Kelly said it was okay and she understood about what he had been going through, and since Vegas as was just a few hours' drive from California, it would be nice to meet finally.

Although they had been speaking for over a decade long, Gianni never had any interest in Kelly other than as a friend, and he was not attracted to her—she simply was not his type. A few days before the Vegas trip, Kelly called up Gianni to say, "You know, I just realized I invited myself on your trip. Are you okay with me being there also and hanging out with you?"

Gianni said he did not mind her coming along and that it would be nice to meet face-to-face, but he told her that "No matter what, we are just friends." This was not a meeting of any potential relationship other than being platonic friends. He wanted to make sure she did not get any ideas in her head about this being more than them meeting, and he said between what recently had happened with his friends, work, and women recently, the last thing he needed was any additional drama involving a woman and potential relationships. She said she was good with that setup, and they were only meeting as friends and nothing else. Unfortunately for Gianni, Kelly decided during the trip—or perhaps her mind was already made up when she decided to meet him—that she did not intend to keep the deal of just meeting as friends. She decided that it was time to tell Gianni what she was feeling.

They were walking around one of the casinos, when all of a sudden she said, "Hey, let's sit down. I want to tell you something."

Well, Gianni got suspicious of this move. She then told Gianni that she liked him very much and was very much attracted to him and would like to be more than just friends. Although Gianni was kind of expecting her to say something like that because of her saying "I want to talk to you," and although he kind of saw it coming, he was still surprised.

Gianni responded with "Kelly, I am sorry. But I do not feel the same way about you as you feel about me." He could see how disappointed she was with his answer, and it was a good thing that it was the last night of their trip when she mentioned it to him because at least the following morning they would both be heading home. Although they remained friends a few more weeks by talking on the phone, you could cut the tension during their conversations. She was not happy about Gianni rejecting her advances, and so he finally told her that they needed to move on because their friendship had been changed and ruined. He said to her, "I told you we were only hanging out as friends, but you still insisted on telling me how you really felt about me. And because I did not feel the same way, it pissed you off, and it pissed me off. You went down that road, and that changed the whole dynamic of our friendship."

CHAPTER 7

After the many years of disappointments for Gianni, he felt like he was never going to meet the girl of his dreams, so he decided to just simply not get worked up about something not working out for him, or to go all in with his emotions to be let down once again. Gianni had decided many years ago after the heartaches and breakups that he no longer would pass up on sex with a woman because he wanted to build a serious relationship. He just decided it was time to go with the flow of the situation. He continued to try and meet girls, but more to see how things would turn out—that was his approach. One of the girls he met turned out to be a girl by the name of Rosa, and she was a newly divorced woman with a newborn baby, so she did not have the time to take on a full-time relationship, but she found Gianni very attractive.

Gianni thought she was attractive but felt that something was missing from her for him to continue to go out with her. She continued to make arrangements to meet up with Gianni, and he told her after a couple dates that he felt like she was too reserved for what he wanted from a woman at this point in his life. And something must have clicked because she began to say that she could definitely be less reserved and share her naughty thoughts she was having about him and her together. Gianni was not sure if she would be capable of delivering the goods, but he decided to see her again and see how things would develop. They made plans for their third date, and she said on Saturday morning/afternoon that she would be moving and be moving closer to where Gianni lived. And if he wanted to get together after, she would like to see him.

Gianni then told Rosa to let him know when she was done, and they would figure out if they would go out and get a bite to eat or see what else they would be doing, depending on how late she would be available or how tired she was from all the moving. He got a call from her around 5:00 p.m., and then she said that she had gone back to pick up the last boxes at her old place to bring over to her new place, but that her friend she was temporarily staying with was out. She could not get a hold of her friend, and her friend was not due back home until after 10:00 p.m. There was a rainstorm going on, and she got caught in it and was soaking wet and could not get inside her new place because she did not have keys yet. And Gianni said, "Wow, talk about bad luck."

He told Rosa, "Well, since you are close by me, you can come over and get out of your soaking wet clothes, and I can throw them in the dryer for you and get you a robe while your clothes dry."

Rosa said to Gianni, "Please don't judge how I am looking, since I got caught in the storm and been sweating all day from moving stuff."

Gianni told Rosa not to worry and that he understood, and she better hurry up, or she might get sick in her wet clothes. A few minutes later, she showed up, and as she said soaking and dripping wet from the rain, since it was still raining. And then Gianni told Rosa, "Here is a fresh towel. If you want to shower, you are more than welcome to use my shower. I don't have clothes that fit you, but maybe I can get you a T-shirt for you to wear and a robe over it. And in the meanwhile, I will get your wet clothes in the dryer, and also I will order us a pizza for delivery for dinner while you are showering."

She said thanks for understanding the situation and sorry for ruining their night out. He said that it was fine since it was pouring outside, and staying in for pizza was just as good an evening as going out. The pizza arrived, and they sat at the dining room table, and they ate the food and spoke some more. And Gianni tried to break the ice a little and said, "So how was your day?"

They both laughed, and then Gianni cleared the table. As he returned to the table, they talked some more, and she said she was very grateful to him for letting her come over to get cleaned up and feed her and everything. He said it was no problem, and then she got up off her chair and said, "Well, maybe I can repay you for your generosity." And then she sat on his lap and began kissing him passionately. And before he knew it, they were having sex on his dining room table. Then they moved over to his couch and then onto the floor and finally ending up in his bedroom and continuing on in there until she could go to her new place when her friend returned home.

This relationship between Rosa and Gianni ended up one between friends with benefits. A relationship together wherein he never got emotionally attached to her. They had agreed that if either one met someone else to date or was dating anyone or someone else, that they would not engage in any sexual activity together so they could pursue or build on the person they were dating. Rosa and Gianni had good sexual chemistry together, and eventually she ended up moving out of state. From that point, the only time they would be having sex was if either one were visiting the other in their home state. Gianni continued to try other dating apps and continued to get the same results: one date and nothing would come out of it, and so on and so on.

He was starting to get bored because he was not dating anyone, and Rosa was no longer someone he saw often, and so he decided to give the dating apps a try again. He could not believe this one website, with women from all over the world: many beautiful women from South America, Europe, and Asia and all attractive. A couple women he began communicating with were telling him that he was such a good-looking man and so nice and so much different from the others. They would start suggesting that they were willing to meet him in person. The problem was they were far and international. Maybe in the back of his mind, he was thinking he might find another woman like Nadia. He continued to chat with a couple of the women from the dating app, and he figured that he had nothing to lose. After all, what was the harm of talking to women internationally? They were from all over the world, and some were living in very poor conditions in Colombia or the Ukraine or Romania or the Philippines, and surely he didn't see himself going to these countries to meet them.

What he did not count on was the fact that these women were willing to pack up and move to the USA for the right man, and they were not shy about what they were expecting from him. One of the women he chatted with frequently online was Sabrina, and she was from Romania. She was attractive and sweet and kind to Gianni when they spoke. She told him she spoke English, Italian, and Romanian—all these languages she learned from going to school. She always had a special liking to Italian men, and Gianni was no exception to her liking. They spoke for about a year online and eventually began to speak by phone video chat. They were now friends moving from online to video/phone, and she hinted she had hoped to one day meet a man from the site for a potential mate. As logical as Gianni has been in his life, he had one thing going against him sometimes, and that was his trusting nature, and he began to feel that trust with Sabrina. The trust he felt was so strong that he began to let his guard down a little and started to think that yes, maybe it was okay to meet her in person. After all, they were friends, and she seemed genuine and nice with Gianni. And because he had her phone number, he began to feel safer about the idea of meeting Sabrina in person. Although he started to consider the idea of meeting Sabrina, he still was not sure if he would actually go through with it. And would he feel secure about the idea of meeting from so far away? But this time he would be the one traveling a long way over to meet her.

He started thinking: how could he meet someone from so far away a place and yet still feel secure about it at the same time? And he began to think about Nadia and how she was from Asia and how he managed to meet her. He began to think about all the girls he had met from online in person from his past and began to remember the failed and successful meetings. And then he began to recall his only international meeting he had in the past, which was Nadia. Gianni began comparing the circumstances between Nadia and Sabrina, and the main difference was the fact that Nadia visited the United States, and he did not have to go someplace he was not familiar with all by himself.

Gianni kept thinking to himself that if he were to meet her, he would be meeting this woman whom he was now friends with, one that he had started chatting with online from the dating site and see how things would turn out for them. But he was hoping it would turn out really good for them. At this point, neither one had made any sort of promise to each one another other than to be open to the possibility of the two of them meeting face-to-face one day. He began thinking about the fact that she was in Romania and he was in the United States. How was this possible? For the two of them to meet? She would not be coming to the United States. Or would she insist that he must come to Romania to meet her?

He began tossing the idea if she was open to the idea of meeting in a neutral place outside Romania and outside the United States. And she said she was open to the suggestion. With that, he then began to wonder: where would this neutral location be for both, for them to feel comfortable to meet one another? He told her he would do some research, and he would get back to her on where the neutral location would be for them to meet.

He started to remember that she said she spoke English and Italian and Romanian and began to think about locations where they could meet where the language spoken was either Italian or English, since Gianni did not speak Romanian. He began to eliminate Australia and England and Ireland, especially since Australia would be too far to go. He contacted his cousin in Italy, Giuseppe, and began to tell him that he was considering meeting a woman for a couple days but was trying to figure out where a good neutral place would be for both him and her. Giuseppe was concerned about his cousin's safety because him being in Italy, they tend to hear the stories coming out of other European nations, and Romania was no exception with bad things that have occurred to people going there. Gianni told Giuseppe that he had met the woman through a dating website but he also did not want him to be overly concerned about how he initially met her and wanted his cousin to focus on a good place to meet someone. Giuseppe then told his cousin to throw the suggestion of meeting in Sardinia, and if she would be open to the idea it would be a neutral site for both.

Gianni then asked his cousin why he picked Sardinia, and Giuseppe then told him it was close enough to Sicily that he and their cousin Luigi could keep an on eye on Gianni, and that was the only way they could ensure his safety. Plus, Giuseppe said that he and Luigi could take a ferry to Sardinia, and when Gianni was done meeting with this girl, the three of them could take a ferry back to Sicily. He could then spend some time in Sicily before Gianni returned home to America. Gianni told Giuseppe that meeting her in Sardinia was a fantastic idea, and he would feel more at ease knowing his family would be nearby. He would run the idea over to Sabrina to see if she would agree to meet there. Once again Gianni, although he was much older at this point in his life, still had people who would be looking after him or keeping an eye on him to protect him, even though he did not request his cousin to do that for him. His family and friends have always been his protectors.

Gianni reached out to Sabrina to float the proposal of meeting in Sardinia Island, not far from Romania and not far from Sicily where he would be heading to after their meeting in Sardinia. She said she thought it was a fantastic neutral spot, and she had always wanted to go to Italy, and Sardinia would be a great start for her! Sabrina then proceeded to ask when they would be meeting, and Gianni said he would have to get back to her on the proposed dates to meet, but he wanted to check with her first and see if Sardinia was okay with her. But now he needed to check with his work schedule to confirm when he could take time off to meet her.

Which was true—he needed to check with his supervisor to make sure he could take time off of work, but he also was looking to coordinate with cousins Giuseppe and Luigi and make sure they could meet Gianni when he arrived in Sardinia to meet Sabrina. The last couple weeks of July were looking like the best time for Gianni to take time off work and to also have his cousins meet him in Sardinia. And so he then told Sabrina when the best dates for him would be. And she responded to Gianni that yes, she in fact could meet him at the proposed dates. A couple days later, Sabrina threw a wrench at Gianni and at the plans of meeting and then proceeded to tell him that yes, she could meet him on the days he was suggesting and would like to meet him in Sardinia, but since the initial talks they had, she was in a financial crunch and would not be able to buy air-fare and pay for her hotel room even if it was only a few short days. Gianni was so let down by this bit of news. He had started building up excitement that they would be meeting, and his cousins would be there to keep an eye on him. He always had a steadfast rule to never send anyone overseas money, so now what would he do? Go on to Sardinia as planned and just be with his cousins? Sabrina told him how sorry she was for letting him down and that she really wanted to meet him in person but that she hoped he would understand her situation.

The plan to meet Sabrina in Sardinia had seemed to come to a screeching halt for Gianni, and he was debating whether there was a viable option so that they could still meet in person. But at what cost would it be? That was the question. Although Gianni had a steadfast rule about never sending money to anyone overseas, especially to someone he never met before, he was trying to figure out if there was a way to meet the financial obligations for Sabrina. His generous nature would sometimes get in his way of logical thinking. He knew that if he sent her money directly, there was no assurance that she would even use the funds to buy airfare to Sardinia. He then suggested to Sabrina if she were to purchase the airfare and then when they met up in Sardinia, he could give her the cash at that point to pay for her airfare and for her hotel.

She told Gianni that she would have to think about it because no man had ever been so generous with her before, and she needed a little while to mull it over before giving him her final answer of accepting or declining his offer. After a couple of days, Sabrina came back with her answer to Gianni and told him she would love to accept his generous offer but that she had no credit line that could cover the charge of the airfare, nor did she have the funds to pay by cash. Gianna began to get frustrated and finally caved in to the idea of sending her the cash by Western Union. Based on the currency rate exchange from US dollars to Romanian leu, he was going to have to put up 1,600 US dollars so she could pay for her flight. He took the big step and went ahead and confirmed her banking information, so he could transfer her the funds to her bank account. She confirmed she received the funds and now would purchase the ticket for the flight. She even went ahead and took screenshots of the flight ticket she was purchasing, so Gianni would know she was using the funds as was planned. And with that, he felt that in just a few short weeks he would be meeting Sabrina for a vacation on the beach. And who knows how things would turn out?

The time finally arrived to go to Sardinia, and he had booked a room for himself and for Sabrina. He gave her the hotel information, so she would check in when she arrived, and then they could meet. She was scheduled to arrive on a Friday, but Gianni decided to arrive on Thursday so he could get himself adjusted with the time difference between the US and Europe. His cousins would be arriving Friday morning. He would meet up with them and go over the plans, so that they would be able to keep an eye out for him.

Gianni headed out to the airport to leave for Italy, and he sent text messages to Sabrina and his cousins to tell them what his status was. His cousins replied fairly quickly and told him that they were looking forward to seeing him soon, but Sabrina did not respond—at least not right away—and so he was at the airport gate waiting anxiously for Sabrina to reply to his text, but still nothing. And so he boarded the plane, and off he was on his first leg to Italy. Throughout the flight he started getting a bad feeling in his gut about Sabrina and actually meeting her. He began to feel that something was amiss and that they would not actually meet, but he left hope for the possibility that maybe he was just paranoid and that maybe she wasn't able to respond until after he got on his fight. Then he would have a message on his phone when he landed, and so this anxiety he was having made the flight feel like it was taking longer than normal to arrive in Italy.

He landed in Rome, and he turned his phone on to check for messages. And sure enough he had messages, but none of the messages were from Sabrina, and not surprisingly at this point—but he decided since he had another couple hours' flight from Rome to Sardinia, he would call Sabrina after he checked in at the hotel. He got to the hotel and checked in and then headed into his room and put his luggage down and grabbed his phone. Still there was no message from Sabrina, and so he called her. The next day, in the afternoon, she was supposed to be on her way to airport. Or at least that was what the plan was. As he pressed her name to call her, he got the message that the call could not go through as dialed. And so he thought that was an *uh-oh* moment, but he dialed again.

Even though he had seen a confirmation about her flight being booked, he went back to his e-mails and checked that e-mail confirmation again. Yes, it was for a flight to Italy, and the dates they agreed on, but then he looked a little more carefully and noticed that it was an information of confirmation right before someone clicks to buy the actual flight. He got that bad feeling in the pit of his stomach and dropped down on the seat of his pants on the bed, and he knew he was duped and would never see her, and he knew he was taken for 1,600 US dollars. He just shook his head in disbelief, but there was nothing he could do about this.

The next morning, his cousins arrived, and they met Gianni at the piazza where he was drinking his cappuccino. They began to ask how things were going and what was happening. He told his cousins that he thought she was scheduled to arrive this afternoon, but he doubted very much that she would be arriving, and he continued on telling them how he could no longer get a hold of her by phone and that she e-mailed him some fake information and conned him out of some cash and that was in fact the endgame for her. One of his cousins said, "Well, shit happens." Things could have actually been much worse than losing a few dollars in the process. And it was good that he was not harmed physically and still had the rest of his life to live. And also, he shouldn't forget that he had a weekend plus all the next week to spend with his cousins and his family in Sicily! Gianni laughed and told his cousins that they were right and in reality he had it in the back of his mind that he didn't really think he would actually meet her, and they were also right about how it was only money he lost—after all, he had heard other stories where people lost more than money. And now it was time to start having fun with his cousins and Sardinia for a few days, and he would quickly get over this episode in his life!

For many years, Gianni never heard much news in regards to what happened with Stephanie. Like, did she get married or have kids and so forth? But typical of Gianni, he did not feel that it was his business after their breakup or at least after he moved on. He felt that the only way to heal was to move on and not concern himself with what his ex was up to. He did not believe in staying friends with someone that he was in a relationship with. Not that he wanted to be enemies with anyone. Nor did his breakups result in bad blood, and that was why he never heard any updates about her.

Later in his years, he became friends with a group of guys that happened to go to the same school as Stephanie and her brother. In fact, they knew her brother from school, a brother who was the same age as Gianni and his friends. As Gianni got to learn about these guys, he would ask little questions about where they went to school or who they knew. And this was how he discovered that they were familiar with her or at least her brother. One day, one of these friends, Phil, e-mailed Gianni to ask him if he was the one who told him about the one who had dated the sister of Nick—the friend that he had gone to school with? Gianni replied to Phil to tell him that yes, in fact he did date Nick's sister. Phil replied back with "That is what I thought." He wanted to let Gianni know that he ran into his ex-girlfriend's husband, and they were talking about his brother in-law, Nick, and somehow he mentioned that he thinks that his buddy Gianni dated his wife prior to the two them getting together. Then Phil also said he would give him all the details when he'd see him at the poker game next week.

Gianni showed up for the poker game, and he asked Phil, "How does something like me dating someone even come up in a conversation?" Phil told Gianni that he was in a meeting with the husband on some business, and they began to speak about where they grew up and what school they went to, and then he asked if Phil knew Nick, who was his wife's brother. And they all went to the same school, and then Phil said that that was how he mentioned he didn't know his wife but that his good friend Gianni had dated her back in the day.

Gianni then responded with "Oh okay, now it makes sense."

Then Phil said, "Oh yeah, he said he remembers you."

And Gianni then said, "Yeah, wait, what?"

Phil said, "Yeah, he said he remembers you would come over where Stephanie worked at."

And although Gianni had a good idea who the husband was based on his suspicions, when he broke it off with her, he was still not 100 percent sure, since he never knew any boyfriend of hers.

So then he then asked Phil what he looked like. Phil described him, but before he started to tell Gianni, he was almost certain what or who Phil was about to describe, and it was as if someone had just punched Gianni in the gut. He got a sick feeling because it brought up the sad memory of the breakup, and it hit him at the same time that he was right about being suspicious initially of this guy, and that was well over twenty years ago when he had that gut feeling at the time when things were going sour for him and Stephanie. And that this guy might play a factor someday, as if Gianni could see the future, so he then told Phil that yes, he now remembers him also.

About a year passed after the episode in Sardinia. Gianni decided that it was time to hang up the dating shoes and just focus on living out the rest of his life in a not-so-dangerous lifestyle and enjoy life by being with his family and friends and going golfing and traveling. His recent investments had resulted in gains that grew his portfolio to proportions where he could start planning on retiring early in a couple short years and comfortably to a point where money was not going to be an issue for him. His professional background in finance helped him with being wise and logical with his investments and his money. He wanted to retire elsewhere, away from Chicago, and perhaps away from the United States as well. He felt that he needed to get away from all the heartache he had gotten from here. He began to explore his options. He was considering places like Costa Rica or Ecuador or Belize or Italy as some of his options. He wanted to move where he knew the weather would not include a brutal winter like Chicago can get at times, and so warmer climates was his first choices.

He called up his cousins in Italy and asked if they knew of some land that was for sale, so he might build his retirement home on. And they told him to just come and visit, and they would take him to some spots that were for sale. Gianni bought his plane ticket to Italy, and the day came, and he headed out to the airport. First, he checked his bags and then headed over to clear security and said goodbye to his family that drove him to the airport. He told them that he would see them all in a couple weeks when he returned. He got through security and then took a seat at the gate, waiting until it was time to board. As he was waiting, he could not help but notice this woman sitting a few seats away. He could swear she looked so familiar to him, but because he could not get a clear view of her face, he wasn't sure if it was his imagination.

As he sat reading his e-mails and text messages on his smartphone, he noticed a shadow over him. As he looked up to see who was standing over him, sure enough he saw that it was that woman from a few seats away. She said, "Gianni, is that you?"

Gianni looked and recognized her voice and realized that it was Renee, his old friend from Jacques School! Gianni got up and said, "Oh my god, Renee, long time no see." And they gave each other a big hug hello. "Last time we saw each other was in college. What are you doing here?" She said she was waiting to board the flight to go to Italy, and what was he doing there? He said he was going to Italy also! He then said, "What a small world we live in, that we are on the same flight to Italy."

And then he asked her who she was traveling with. She said no one, that she was traveling alone. Her kids had bought her a travel package to Italy. "And what about you? Who are you traveling with?"

He told her he bought his own ticket to Italy but that he would be meeting his cousins in Italy, and she said, "Of course, Mr. Italian, you have family in Italy."

She told him she had never been to Italy but always wanted to go, so her kids bought her a package. Gianni then said, "Wow, you look like you did when I saw you last. It's like you barely aged."

And she said, "Well, what about you? Look at you: no gut, still athletic and muscular shaped, and you don't look your age one bit!"

Gianni then laughed and said, "What is your seat number?"

She said, "Why are you asking?"

He said, "Because I think I know the answer already."

And then she laughed because she also just realized what he was saying and looked at her ticket: 1B.

And he laughed. "*Of course*, I am 1A. We are going to be sitting next to each other for eight hours! Talk about getting a chance at catching up over a few hours. This was the first flight in a long time that he was looking forward to flying, especially a flight this long! Renee was delighted also and said this would be a fun flight. And it would probably be over before they get done talking and catching up.

They sat down in their seats and began to talk as if they were best friends. Gianni continued to tell her that he could not believe the odds of them meeting like this again—the odds were, like, almost astronomical! He then asked her, "Are you sure you can handle being on a long flight like this?"

She then said, "Well, what do you mean? Why don't you think I could handle the long flight?"

"Oh," he said, "if I recall correctly, you smoke. And there is no smoking during the flight."

And she laughed. "I stopped smoking when I got pregnant with my first child."

And she then proceeded to also to tell him she had three kids, and she been divorced for the past five years. She waited to divorce until her kids were old enough, especially after her third child was born. After that, she decided it was time to divorce her husband. And here she was, now a divorced mom of three wonderful kids and leading a happy life. And now she was heading to Italy, a place that had been on her bucket list since she was a child. And now she was on a plane sitting next to her old friend, who was bringing back wonderful memories of their childhood!

Gianni said he was sorry to hear she was divorced, and Renee said she was not sorry and wanted him to be happy for her. Gianni then said, "Okay, congratulations," with a big smile on his face!

Then Renee asked Gianni, "What is the scoop with you? What happened? Did you ever marry? Have kids?"

Gianni then laughed and said, "It is a good thing we have a very long flight." It was a long flight for him to tell her his story, and so he proceeded to tell Renee about Stephanie and how he thought he was going to end up getting married and having a family and how things ended and how things have been a struggle for him in the love and relationship department.

Renee then said, "She told you she was afraid you would cheat on her because all men eventually cheat?"

Gianni then said, "Yeah that's what she said." But he added that recently he found out some things about her and that her fear of him cheating was just a bullshit excuse so that she wouldn't admit that she was about to start a relationship with someone she ended up getting married with. Renee said yes, it sounded like a bullshit excuse to her also, and maybe she had already cheated on him. Renee said the Gianna she grew up to know and became friends with was not a bad guy and was one of the sweetest and nicest guys she ever knew, not the type of guy that would cheat or lie or be dishonest. She continued on to tell him, "When I saw you in college, and I see you now, it is like you didn't change. Still the same sweet and smiling and happy Gianni. That's what makes you so attractive!"

Gianni then proceeded to ask Renee if he could ask what led to her divorce. This was a man she had known since high school. Renee then told him yes, he could ask and she would be glad to tell him. She told him, "When we are young and we fall in love with someone, there a lot of things we miss or overlook about our partner. Some things are subtle, and some things are obvious to others. But some things are not so obvious to others. But in any case, I basically forgave him for a lot of his shortcomings because I loved him. And well, when you love someone you tend to forgive them and continue on with the relationship. Can I be blunt with you, Gianni?"

Gianni told her, "Yes, of course, be as honest as you want."

And she on went to say, "After many years of being in a relationship with someone who stopped loving me or showing me he loved me, he never said it anymore. He didn't show it to me or express it to me by the way he treated me. He was rather cold to me as if I was no longer at top of his priority list of importance, and I was at the very bottom. Those were some of his shortcomings. And then of course when you are with a partner that doesn't show you love or expresses their love to you, and when he wants sex it was only when he wanted sex. And when he did want sex, it was not very good sex and only focused on him getting off and never concerned about what I wanted or how I would like to maybe feel special or be seduced. For him it was *wham*, *bam*, thank you, ma'am. And it was over in the blink of an eye. I was never even turned on by his actions. And good thing they have toys for women, otherwise I would had been even more miserable than I already was. And so I finally had enough. And that is my story."

Gianni told her he was shocked. And Renee asked him why he was shocked. "Well, for years I have heard about men like your ex-husband. But I never understood those kinds of guys. And probably I could never understand men like that because I am not like that at all. Sorry, but I believe it is all about the respect you give and show your partner. That will give you the best results in the relationship. Honestly, Renee, I don't care how long I have been with my partner. No way would, all of a sudden, I would just not have interest in showing her love or being loving to her or being selfish in the relationship. But hey, that's me and I can't speak for others. I just know that if I were in a relationship with you, I probably would not keep my hands off you and certainly would continuously find ways to seduce you, keep it fresh as they say, and never fall in the same rut!"

Renee then told Gianni, "You know, I believe that about you. I really truly believe that you would not be selfish. I bet that this is how you've been throughout all your relationships over the years."

Gianni said, "Yeah, I am not a selfish man, not a selfish lover, not a selfish anything. And I believe in expressing or showing my love to my partner." Gianni then said to Renee. "Let's exchange phone numbers, and when we get back to Chicago we can get together and continue to catch up?"

Renee said, "I was thinking the same thing. It will be nice to continue to catch up on the old days and how life has been in between until now!"

They landed and went their separate ways, but now he had a new spring in his step. And as he was walking toward the next flight to get to Sicily, he then could not help but think of the song that was most fitting for this moment for Renee. And he began to think about the song "Fantasy Girl" by Johnny O. Many of the lyrics in the song he felt was definitely fitting for her and the situation, although the meaning of this song was very accurate about his feelings and the situation itself. He also wanted to be careful because he did not want to start celebrating and start spiking the football in the end zone, since at this point they only agreed to exchange numbers and to get together and catch up some more. But maybe, just maybe, this was the last time he would have to look for someone.

There is an old saying that it will happen when you least expect it. And he certainly was not expecting this whatsoever. And now he had a couple of weeks to plan on the next get-together with Renee. This time he did not forget to ask for a girl's phone number and was the aggressive one when he had that chance encounter! It is funny how life seems to start one way and then life moves on and changes toward another point in your life. And then it circles right back on to where it started in the first place.

REFERENCES

New Edition. "Cool It Now." MCA Records, 1984.

A Flock of Seagulls. "I Ran (So Far Away)." Jive Records, 1982.

Christopher Cross. "Ride Like the Wind." Warner Records, 1979.

Kool & the Gang. "Fresh." *The Very Best of Kool & the Gang.* UMG Recordings, 1999. CD.

Bay City Rollers. "You Made Me Believe in Magic." *It's a Game.* Arista Records, 1977.

Foreigner. "Head Games." Atlantic Records, 1979.

Ollie & Jerry. "Breakin'." Polydor, 1984.

Kool & the Gang. "Tonight." *The Very Best of Kool & the Gang.* UMG Recordings, 1999. CD.

Kool & the Gang. "Misled." The Very Best of Kool & the Gang. UMG Recordings, 1999. CD.

The Alan Parsons Project. "Games People Play." *The Turn of a Friendly Card.* RCA Records, 1980. Album.

Timex Social Club. "Rumors." *Vicious Rumors.* Fantasy Records, 1986. Album.

Sweet Sensation. "Take It While It's Hot." ATCO Records, 1988. CD.

Kool & the Gang. "Tonight." *The Very Best of Kool & the Gang.* UMG Recordings, 1999. CD.

Stevie B. "Spring Love." *Party Your Body.* LMR Records, 1988. CD.

Johnny Hates Jazz. "Shattered Dreams." Virgin Records, 1987.

TKA. "Scars of Love." Tommy Boy Records, 1987. CD.

Stevie B. "Girl I am Searching for You." *In My Eyes.* LMR Records, 1988. CD.

B-Cap. "Send Me An Angel." Key One Records, 1995. CD.

Lou Rawls. "You'll Never Find Another Love Like Mine." *All Things in Time.* Philadelphia International Records, 1976. CD.

Eagles. "One of These Nights." Asylum Records, 1974. CD.

Johnny O. "Fantasy Girl." Micmac Records, 1988. Vinyl.

ABOUT THE AUTHOR

Massimo Parlermo grew up in Chicago and is part of Generation X. He grew up in a first-generation Italian American family. When he began attending grammar school, Italian was the first language he spoke and had the task of learning a new language, English. After completing grade school and high school, he then went on to college. He graduated from Purdue University Global with a degree of bachelor of science in business administration, magna cum laude. His professional career has been spent in business in the field of finance and accounting, with him working in many various business settings over the years. While growing up, his favorite sports were baseball, football, and basketball, but essentially he liked just about every sport. In his free time, these days he enjoys spending time with his family and friends and enjoys golfing and traveling along with sharpening his cooking skills by trying out and cooking new recipes. He enjoys watching classic movies with actors like Humphrey Bogart, James Stewart, Gary Cooper, Marilyn Monroe, and Jane Russell. He enjoys listening to all different genres of music, starting from the 1950s and up to the music going on today.

Desire for Love is the first book he has written, and the subject of the book is about love and relationships. This is certainly a subject he felt that most readers could relate to.